The Fire

In

The Dark

By: Tessa L. Gatz

Acknowledgements

Thank you to all those that had
helped me write this book. Thank you to my family especially
my mom for all that she does for me.
I would also like to thank my English teacher Miss Smith, and
my friends
Caitlin Prindle, Jacy Ayers, Megan Honeycutt, Marla Villaruel
and Nicole Prindle
For encouraging me and being there for me and making this
book what it is today.

Table of Contents

Tessa L. Gatz

Chapter 1

The Arrival

It's a blazing summer afternoon, with a slight breeze that brings a refreshing smell of flowers. There's a swing set moving ever so slightly that it could have been imagined. The house is modern, in an idealistic way. It is a two-story house with just enough room for my family, which consists of Grandma Gin, Mama June, Uncle Larry, and my two brothers, Josh and John. My Grandfather died a few months after Mama June was born. Grandma Gin never actually talks about him just, as my Mom never talks about my dad. We call him JD, John Doe. He disappeared almost instantly after I was born, at least that's what my brother Josh tells me every time I ask. I'm 16 years old and the youngest in my family. I take after my mother more than anything. I have long brown hair with natural highlights that gives my hair a natural shine. My eyes are a greenish gold, and my skin is bronze. I'm five foot four. Mama June is five eleven, she works nights as a nurse, so my grandma and my brothers usually take care of me. While Uncle Larry usually watches Tv and drinks.

This afternoon is a different story, Uncle Larry lifts himself off the crusty old couch and rushes to the bathroom. After thirty minutes he reappears. His silver hair slicked back with a thick layer of goo, he is in a black suit with a blood red tie and silver cufflinks.

"Okay, I'm going out," Larry said with a crooked smirk. He rushed out the door before I could even get a word out. Where is he going? I thought, as I sit beside the window. But as everything goes, I lost interest in the thought. Especially when I saw that John had arrived.

"Well, hello there kiddo!" John dropped his suitcases on the ground and wrapped his long awkward arms around me.

"Too tight. Can't…. Breath." I tried to say as I gasp for air.

"Ooh sorry kiddo. I'm just so excited to see you!" He chuckled while adjusting his thick-rimmed glasses. "It's been five months. Aren't you excited to see me?"

"Of course, I am," I said with a smile that seems to make John's greenish-hazel eyes light up with partial joy, for the other part is sadness, which I'd never seen before. John has always been considered as the happy one in our family, for the only time I've ever seen him cry was when he was pushed to the ground and my oldest brother had to recuse him.

"What's wrong John? Did something happen while you were away?" I spoke softly with a hint of urgency.

He ran his hand nervously through his dark dirty blond hair and looked into my eyes while halfway opening his mouth as if he's going to tell me a secret, but then quickly changed his mind.

"Nothing," John spoke with a barely noticeable sigh. His eyes deepened, and he withdrew. "Where is everyone?" John asked as though I didn't notice that he changed the conversation.

"Grandma Gin is in the kitchen, Mama is resting in her room, Uncle Larry left about an hour ago, and Josh is at work. He should be home in time for dinner."

"Okay, well I'm going to get cleaned up, then we can go and sit on the deck and talk about how you've been doing, and how the old family is holding up. Okay?" He smiled.

"Fine," I said with an eye roll. He pulled me in for a quick embrace before starting to walk to the bathroom. Before he entered he turned around and smiled.

"Also, can you do me a favor?"

"Depending on what it is." My eyebrow floated up in interest.

"Can you take my bags to my room please." He said it with a begging smile.

"Sure, but on one condition" I replied with a laugh

"Name it."

"One word." I grinned suspiciously, "ice cream"

He nodded his head in agreement before disappearing behind the door. While I laughed I lugged each suitcase up the stairs to John's room. In his room one wall is a library of books, while the bed faced the door, and the desk covered with papers faced the window.

I set his suitcases on his bed. Just as I was about to walk out of the room I saw out of the corner of my eye a picture peeking from the corner pocket of his suit case. There's a man in the picture. The man has dark hair and olive-toned skin. His eyes look to be green, his beard is thick and messy. The man's surrounded by mountains with a small hut in the background. I was about to turn the picture over, when I heard footsteps approaching. As I rush to put it back in the suitcase. The steps grew closer and closer. I could hear my heartbeat rapidly increasing. I fumbled with the picture, as the door creaked open.

"Thank you for hauling my stuff to my room." John's voice is light. My eyes followed him to his bed where the pocket was still unzipped with a corner of the picture still peeking out.

"No problem, do you need help unpacking?" I said eagerly, in hope that I could confront him about the picture I found.

"No," He said hastily, "I mean, I can do it. There's a lot of stuff and I have to organize it but thank you." John smiled and gave me a secure nod.

"Well, okay then. I'll see you downstairs" I gave him a smile, then walked quickly out of the room, and down the stairs. Thoughts are rushing through my brain. The question that replayed in my mind throughout the afternoon was; Who is the man in the picture?

John and I sat outside and talked until dusk. I would have never noticed if Mama June didn't shriek.

"Awwwww John, you're home! When did you arrive?" She said in an exhilarating tone.

"Hello, mother. I arrived around noon." John laughed and gave her a huge hug that made her cry. They weren't sad tears, but instead, they were happy tears.

"I missed you so much."

"I missed you too" John whispered in a loving voice.

"I have to go to work, but we'll talk later?" Mama June said, reassuring herself and John.

"Yes, Mama June. We will." He said as if there was an unspoken meaning, a code like the Navajo used. I learned about the Navajo before summer vacation. The Navajo code was used in World War II by the U.S to send encrypted messages. The Navajo code is uncrackable still to this day. I couldn't help thinking this has something to do with the John being gone.

"Jacy? Jacy? Hello?" He waved his hand in front of my face.

"Hmm, Oh hello John." I laughed, "Look there's Josh." Josh is the oldest out of the three of us. His skin is like an olive gold that reflects in his eyes and complements his dark brown hair. He's about six foot with an athletic build, which accommodated him when he participated in basketball and football. Which is the complete opposite of John.

Josh drove up in an old red farm truck. When he exited the car he was wearing a navy-blue jumpsuit, with a permanent smell of sweat and steel. His hands are covered in a thick black layer of grease and he has smudges on his face. I quickly ran over to greet him.

"Josh you're home!" I smiled.

"Hi Jacy, how was today?" He said with a smile. As we were walking towards the house together.

"A lot happened today," I said with a laugh.

"What happened?"

"Uncle Larry left without saying a word, and John is back." I motioned towards the porch.

Josh looked up at the porch. His face turned stern and his eyes cold as he saw John sitting on the steps. John returned the look, then stood up and walked inside.

"What is that about?" My voice is shaky, and Josh is quiet. There's an absence of sound at this moment. It's like time froze.

"He left us..." Those words hung in the air as we walk slowly up towards the house.

Chapter 2

The Question

That night, Grandma Gin prepared a huge dinner in favor of John's return. She made his favorite dish, turkey with mashed potatoes and a light brown gravy that enhanced the moisture in the turkey, in a way that melts in your mouth. The potatoes are creamy fluffy clouds that bring a comforting warmth to this cold summer evening.

Even though John had been gone for several months we still sit in the same seats every time, as if his ghost still occupied his spot. John sits next to me and on the other side of me is Josh. Mama June is always working, so Grandma Gin sits diagonally from John and across from Uncle Larry, who still hasn't returned from his outing earlier this afternoon. Which is unusual, he never skips a chance to eat Grandma Gins famous turkey. He's probably at the bar downtown and lost track of time. It's refreshing to see John back in his spot, but the tension was boiling up as we sat in silence for the first hour. Well, it was more like five minutes, but it could have been an hour.

"So John, how was your trip?" Grandma Gin said with an uncomfortable voice.

"It was uneventful… but good I traveled to places and learned a lot over these past five months, but I'm glad to be home." John spoke with a smile that said everything will be alright as if something is wrong. I began to think. What happened while he was away?

"What did you do when you were gone?" I inquired.

"I spent time with kids and worked with a charity in Nelspoort, South Africa. It was a life-changing experience," he spoke as if he couldn't reveal too many details about his trip.

"Charity" Josh snorted. Grandma Gin immediately glared at Josh as though she could spank him with her mind. Josh leaned back in his chair trying to escape Grandma Gin's glare.

"What charity?" I asked. John's eyes darted to the left as if he were trying to think of what charity he was with for five months.

"The *Make It Rain* charity. We built wells and helped the children with education and meals." John spoke hesitantly. As though he's unsure if I would believe him.

"That's a good experience for you, John. I'm glad you're back, so now you can help me with the garden." Grandma Gin insisted. John chuckled.

"Okay, Grandma. Okay." John's voice was deep with sarcasm.

I tried a few more conversation starters to break the tension, but all were unsuccessful. We finished dinner in silence.

It's my turn to clean up dinner this week. In my house, we have a revolving chore schedule that was made before I was born. Every week one person makes dinner, while another cleans up, and in the morning and afternoon it's fend for yourself.

"Here I'll help you." Josh smiled and, started by grabbing the glasses while I grabbed the plates.

"Thank you, Josh," I uttered in a wondering voice, for my mind was elsewhere.

"Jacy are you okay?" He mumbled.

"Yes." I lied. I didn't want to put Josh in the same position I'm in. Which is, why is John lying? This question would have angered him, so I lied.

"Okay, what are you doing on Saturday?" Josh changed the topic with a voice full of doubt.

"I'm hanging out with my friends Saturday evening. You can join if you want to hang with a bunch of girls." My voice was light with laughter.

"I think I'll pass but thank you for the offer." Josh came over and gave me a hug and laughed. "I love you."

"Well, thank you, I love me too." We laughed.

After the dishes Josh went to take a shower, John was already in his room, Grandma Gin was watching TV, and Uncle Larry still hadn't returned, this was unusual, but I still didn't think too much of it. As I strolled up to my room, I reflected on today's events. John returning with a mysterious picture and a lie about how he spent his last five months away. The resentment Josh has for John leaving, and how Uncle Larry got up and left looking like a man from the Russian mafia. This was rushing through my head and began to give me a headache.

As I was laying on my bed, reading about Cultures Around The World. Specifically a page about South Africa. When I was exploring it, my phone dinged. I placed my book down slowly as I looked over at my phone to see a text from Luke, and my heart dropped. When I was a freshman there was a new kid, his name was Luke Reynolds. His skin is gold, and his chiseled jaw framed the icebergs that are his eyes and his vigorous body showed through his shirt. When people looked at him they would freeze in awe of his beauty. But as all beauty goes there's a beast, and that's his personality.

'Hey.' His text said. I didn't know what to type. I was shocked that he would text me. Luke's popularity comes from his beauty and athletic ability, and don't forget his smooth talent to talk any girl into bed.

'Hey,' I reply.

'I have a question for you.'

'And that is?' I typed as though I could put emotions into the words.

'Are you friends with Kim?' I rolled my eyes when I looked at his text. I anticipated what he was going to ask for, Kim's number.

'No.' I type, with part-jealousy and part-instinct to protect my friend from becoming a victim. I threw my phone down Then I went back to my book but soon after I fell asleep.

It was around midnight when I heard voices coming from downstairs. I slid out of bed and started to creep down the hall to the top of the staircase.

"What did you find out?" A soft woman's voice spoke.

"It's him." A husky male voice said so quietly that I had to move a couple of stairs down.

"Oh my..." The woman began to cry softly. I tried to get closer to see who was talking.

"What was that?" the man's voice shook. I turn without hesitation and I moved as quickly and as quietly as I could back to my room. I shut the door and hastily crawl under my sheets. Just as the door opened enough for a beam of light to peek through. It disappears as quickly as it appeared. Who was the man? Who was the woman? Who did they find? Why is he important? All these questions made me think back to John. I thought about who it could be. Mama June was at work. It couldn't be her. If not Mama June, then who? And the man, John, but his room is next to mine. I'm a light sleeper so I would be able to hear him if he left his room. Uncle Larry? He was still out by the time I went to sleep. Who were they looking for? Who did they find? These questions tortured me throughout the night. Even in my sleep, they followed me, but the one I fixated on is, Who did they find?

Chapter 3

The Fair

It's a warm Saturday morning. The temperature feels like a mild sixty-five degrees, and the day has just begun. I'm looking forward to getting out of the house and away from John and Josh's constant bickering. Grandma Gin has been trying to keep it under control, but when you put two lions in a room nothing peaceful can come out of it.

This morning I woke up to a slamming door and shouting. I leaped out of bed and rushed to look out the window to see Uncle Larry's face as red as a tomato. I couldn't see, so I adjust my position to try and see who he's yelling at, he turns abruptly, got into his blue pickup, and was gone in a cloud of dust. My mind tingled with questions. I turn towards my door, and walk down the stairs. As I'm about to enter the kitchen, I heard Grandma Gin and Mama June talking.

"He's putting our family in danger." Grandma Gin's voice is filled with fear.

"He's providing some sort of income." Mama June spoke in a soft voice.

"Which he wastes on beer," Grandma said angrily.

"So, at least he's spending his own money, and not ours."

"Yes, but his work could get us …Good morning Josh." Grandma Gin's voice changed from protective and concerned to loving and kind.

"Good morning, Mama June, Grandma Gin," Josh said.

"Good morning, Jacy," John whispered with a laugh. I jumped and socked him in the shoulder.

"Ouch! What was that for?" John laughed while rubbing his shoulder.

"You know what that was for." I crossed my arms, turned and walked into the kitchen, as did John. As soon as Josh saw him his face turned from happy to a mix of anger and sadness.

"John." His sentences are short and abrupt.

"Good morning, Josh," John said with a smug tone. I looked from Josh to John anticipating a fight, but instead, Josh left. I wasn't sure whether he left because of John or because of work. On Saturdays, Josh worked in the mornings at the All Car Shop, and in the afternoon he usually comes home and works on his truck.

"So, what's for breakfast?" John asked in an attempt to break some tension that filled the room.

"Whatever you can make, you can have." Grandma Gin said.

"Okay, do we have cereal?"

"I believe so," I said as I walked over to the pantry. "What kind would you like?"

"What do you have?"

"We have Cocoa Pebbles, Rocky Flakes, and Lucky Cheerios."

"Can I have Rocky Flakes?"

"Hmm, I don't know. That's my favorite kind." I said with a shoulder shrug.

John rolled his eyes and laughed. "Just give me the cereal."

Mama June and Grandma Gin left to sit on the porch. John and I stayed and sat at the kitchen bar.

"What are you going to do today?" I said with a grin.

"I don't know yet." John's eyes looked down at his cereal and his face contorted into a thoughtful look. "What are you going to do?"

"I'm going to hang out with my friends at the fair just out of town."

"That will be fun." His voice filled with forged joy.

"Do you not think it will be fun?" I said with a hostile voice, and John picked up on it.

"No, of course not. It'll be fun." He tried to reassure me. Even though I didn't buy it, I pretended as though I did. I didn't want to fight this early in the morning. I let it roll off my shoulder and continued to eat in silence.

The long intense morning turned into a subtle afternoon. After everyone disbursed into their own agendas for the day, I went to my room to think of Grandma Gin's and Mama June's conversation this morning. Especially how Grandma Gin believed Uncle Larry's job is a danger to our family. How? It's a big question. Uncle Larry is a drunk who could barely do math, unless he has a superpower that gives him the ability to finally be able to walk straight. This thought made me laugh uncontrollably. What could he do that could be so dangerous?

By the time I got done pondering this question, I was late to get ready for the night out with my friends. I hurried to the bathroom, quickly washed up and applied make-up. Then I scurried to my room and got dressed. I put on a casual black sweatshirt with an Adidas sign, I paired this with black leggings and black and white converse. My hair is in a beach wave curl that made it seem as I just got done swimming. I looked over my outfit before I headed downstairs to go out and meet my friends at the fair.

It was nine-thirty when I arrived at the fair. I looked at my phone and saw a text from Kim.

'Hey, Madison and I are by the Ferris Wheel.'

'Okay, I'll be there in five,' I replied. As I'm walking towards the Ferris Wheel, the brisk summer night reminds me of the summer night when Josh and John had set up a tent in the backyard, as a makeshift camping trip. Mama June had to work that night. I was extremely upset when I heard we couldn't go camping. That's when Josh and John set up a fire ring and a tent, which turned out to be the best time of my life. Looking back on that night reminded me of the old Josh and John. How they completed each other, like Pooh and Piglet.

"Jacy! Hey, Jacy! Over here!" I turn to see Kim waving her hand, and beside her, Madison. She was talking to someone on the other side of her. He's tall with dark dirty blond hair, its medium length made it spiral out of control in the summer breeze. As I'm walking over my jaw dropped and I froze, Luke Reynolds.

Chapter 4

Reynolds

I'm frozen like a block of ice. The sight of pretty boy Luke and Madison together is a shock. The day before school got out for summer vacation, Madison confessed about her crush on Luke. I tried to warn her but, obviously, she ignored it.

"Jacy? What are you doing?" Kim said with a subtle laugh.

"I... I... What?" I couldn't comprehend what was going on.

"Hey, Jacy," Luke said with a flirtatious smile.

"Hey," Madison said with a hint of jealousy.

"Hello, Luke, Kim, and Madison." My voice is distant. "Luke, what are you doing here?"

"I was invited by Madison," he said with a smug look. "Why? Do you have a problem with me being here?"

I clench my jaw. "No, of course not. You're totally welcome." Madison and Kim look back and forth between Luke and me. "What are you guys looking at?"

"Nothing." They said simultaneously.

"So, let's get some food. I can't stay this handsome if I don't eat." Luke winks at me and puts his arm around Kim and Madison.

"Okay. Jacy, are you coming?" Madison said, and from there I knew this is going to be a long night.

After walking around for an hour, we finally found a place that Luke wanted to eat at, The Corndog Hut. After we order, we go and sit at one of the tables. Kim sat next to me, across from me is Luke and Madison across from Kim. Luke and Madison are getting on my nerves with her flirting and his ego. It didn't make well for a pleasant evening with my friends.

"What's wrong, princess?" Luke said with a smile.

"Nothing, and don't call me princess," I smile back, but I knew my facial expression said a different story.

"Why not? Princess." He leans slightly towards me and moves his foot over mine. My face flushed with red, and I instantly moved my foot.

"If you call me princess then I'll call you Jabba," I smirk. When we made eye contact his eyes softened, and I felt a sense of yearning. I felt my face growing warmer, and I thought I can't let him win. I broke the connection to return to my food. Still the feeling of his eyes on me, made my stomach turn.

"This is a really good corn dog," Kim said in an uncomfortable tone.

"Yes, it is a very good corn dog," Madison said with contempt.

"So Madison what rides would you like to go on?" Luke said, in an attempt to rapidly change the focus from an awkward-tension-breaker conversation to a friendly one.

"I want to go on the Ferris wheel. What about you?" She smiles.

"Sounds good to me. What about you Jacy, Kim?" He smiles while his eyes darted away from mine.

"I'm fine with it."

"Okay, I'm down," Kim said.

"Kim, guess what," I said excitedly.

"What?" Kim tried to read my face to see if she could guess it.

"John is back."

"John's home! When did he get back?"

"Yesterday." I smile.

"I'll have to stop by and say hi." Kim smiled and laughed. I never knew what happened between Kim and John, but I know it ended as soon as John left for his trip, and Kim was upset.

"John's home?" Madison asked with a smile.

"Yes," I said with a nod.

"We should go in line for the Ferris wheel if we plan on riding it before the night is over," Luke spoke in a low voice, with a smile of anticipation.

"Agreed," I said, as I stood up to throw away my trash. "Are you ready?"

"Yes," they all said.

We started walking towards the Ferris wheel. Luke and Madison are in front of Kim and me. They're talking about sports and Madison is laughing as if everything he says is funny.

I rolled my eyes and kept walking. When we arrive at the Ferris Wheel, the line isn't very long. While we waited about five minutes, Kim and I listen to Luke and Madison conversation. But I zoned out thinking of John's trip and how it has changed him. He's become more secretive which is unsettling. Before John left for his trip, he would always tell me everything, from his first kiss to when his belt broke and his pants fell down in the cafeteria. Now, he won't tell me the truth about what happened in South Africa. If that's really where he was at.

"Next, please." The operator said. We all step up. "Two to a seat."

"I'll sit with Jacy," Luke said. My eyes widen with surprise.

"You should probably go with Madison," I spoke with an insisting voice.

"No, I'll ride with you." He shrugs and smiles. Madison gave me a glare, which I return with an apologetic look. Luke and I got on the ride, and he put his arm around me.

"What are you doing?" I said in an annoyed voice. "Aren't you with Madison?" He nods his head slowly as if he's thinking of what he should say.

"No." He smiles while scooting closer.

"Why are you leading her on then?" I furrow My eyebrows and, I grab his hand, removing his arm from around my shoulders.

"What do you mean?" Luke's face tilted slightly in a questioning matter.

"You know what I mean. By putting your arm around her, chatting her up." My voice is maxed with sass. He opens his mouth then he shuts it as we stop at the top. The view is magnificent. The stars reflecting off the ocean's still bay, and the mountains framing the art that is the world.

"It's beautiful," Luke said, with his blue eyes looking straight at me. I didn't know what to say at first but then I remember Madison and how much she likes him.

"Hmm, sadly my view isn't that beautiful." I chuckled.

Luke smiles and leans in. "That's what you say now but just wait. You'll love me." He whispers seductively. I lean closer until we are breathing the same air.

"I... Don't... Think... So..." I pronounced each word in a breathless whisper, I slowly start to smile, then turn away from him. He smiles with a low laugh.

After the ride, Luke decided to walk me out. Which I didn't agree to but, I also knew if I tried to protest, he wouldn't listen. As we were walking in silence to my car, I saw a man, who looks familiar. As he grew closer and closer, I start to walk closer to Luke as if he could protect me. The man has a thick beard with olive-gold skin.

The man in the picture, he's here. As he walk past, I try to avoid eye contact.

"Excuse me, can you help with directions to the snack shack?" The man said. I freeze and push closer to Luke. His chest was against my back; I can feel his breath getting heavier.

"Yeah, go three blocks down, and it's right on your left," Luke spoke with a new authority.

"Thank you." The man made eye contact with me. His eyes are a greenish-hazel that shows no emotion, like an abyss. Luke looks at me and smiles as a gesture of comfort.

"You alright?" I felt the weight of his hand resting on my waist.

"Yeah, of course." I didn't want to show any more weakness then I already have. I move away from him. Leaving the heat of his hand like an imprint on my waist.

Luke cleared his throat, shoving his hands in his pocket. "Who was that guy?" Luke motions towards the direction the man went.

"I have no idea," I spoke with determination, and, thought I'm going to find out.

Chapter 5

The Clue

It's around eleven o'clock when I return home. I walk in and shut the door gently behind me. I thought back to how Luke showed a vulnerable side, which was a refreshing side to see. My face grew warm thinking of this, but then I quickly remembered Madison and the thought of losing a friend over a boy who I had no interest in. So, I put Luke out of my mind and decided to focus on the man in the picture appearing at the fair tonight. It made me uncomfortable thinking that the man with soulless eyes is associated with my brother John, and I didn't know how to confront John about it. I could march up to his room and talk to him about it now, or I could wait until morning when I have a clear mind. I pondered on these options then decided to wait until morning. I was exhausted, I walked to my room with heavy feet; as soon as my head hit the pillow, I was out.

When I woke up, I tried to decide how to approach John. When I heard the door to John's room open. I slid out of bed, and speed walked to intercept John in the hall.

"John? Can we talk?"

"Sure, what's going on?" His voice sounded intrigued.

"It's about last night?" I said dodging eye contact.

"What about it?"

"I saw a man that looks exactly like someone I've seen in a picture." I smile painfully, my hands fidgeting.

"What picture?" John's voice became stern and full of emotion.

"The picture in your suitcase." John's face drained of color, his eyes were full of emotions, fear, sadness, and concern.

"I gotta go." John ran past me. What is that about? I turn around and rush after him, but it's too late. John is gone.

I sit on the porch looking down the driveway, listening to the birds chirping. There's a wind that brings the smell of fresh rain, which is refreshing considering how hot this summer is. I stared down the way and saw a car. As it's pulling up, I stood up and see who it could be. It's Mama June.

"Hey, sweetie what are you up to?" Mama June came over and wrapped me in her arm. I felt comfortable and safe in her arms; my eyes start to swell with tears.

"Mama June, I think John's in trouble." I wept.

"Oh sweetie, why do you think that?" Her voice is loving and soft.

"Because, in John's suitcase I found a picture of a man and now that man is here, and when I told John about it. He just left." My voice is horse as I attempt to talk and cry at the same time.

"I see, you have nothing to worry about I will talk to him tonight." Her voice changed; it was more distant. She knows something and isn't telling me. I pull away, smile.

"Thank you. I love you." I said.

"I love you too." She kisses my forehead, then walks into the house.

I couldn't shake the feeling that I'm in danger and so is my family. I thought of all the lies; the man in the picture, and Uncle Larry. I never thought that my life could change so drastically when John returned home. What was he doing in South Africa? If that's where he actually was. While I was thinking, my phone dinged.

'Hey, can we talk?' The text was from Madison, I already know what she wants to talk about, Luke.

'Hey, of course. How about we meet up later at the Coffee House?' I typed. I'm worried because, I didn't know what to say.

'Yes! Sounds like a plan. See you at two.'

'See you then,' I reply. It's one o'clock now, so I had thirty minutes to get ready. As I got ready, I began to think of what I would say. I ran every possible point, I don't like Luke, and I never will, or the route of I'm sorry he's just so annoying and I didn't feel like fighting him. Either way, I didn't think she would believe me. I didn't like Luke, he was obnoxious and full of himself, which proved to be true throughout high school when he had a chance to stand up for a kid but instead, he chose his image. That's not a man I want to be with.

When I arrived at the Coffee House, I saw Madison sitting at the table in the corner. I took a breath then walk over.

"Hey, Madison." I smile as I sit down.

"Hi, Jacy. So I want to talk to you about Luke." Her voice lowered as she said his name.

"Yeah, I figured that's what you wanted to talk about. And look I have no feelings for him whatsoever." I put up my hand as a sign of innocence, which I was. Madison laughs.

"I know, I want to know if he said anything about me." She smiles.

"Oh, yes. He asked some questions about you and he said you were nice." I lied through my teeth, but I didn't want to hurt her feelings, for the fact that he said nothing.

"Thank you. So tell me about how life has been with John back home?"

"It's been interesting. He's been lying to me, but so has my whole family."

"About what?"

"About what he was doing when he left, and Uncle Larry apparently has a job that has my whole family in danger. Also, Mama June knows something and won't tell me. The only person I can trust is Josh, but with all things considered he hasn't been around much." I shook my head in frustration.

"Oh wow. You've got a lot going on." Her eyes widened and she laughs.

"Sadly yes." I return the look. We sat and talked about how her crush for Luke has grown stronger and how my life is spiraling out of control.

By the time I got home. John is still gone, and Josh is out. Uncle Larry has disappeared, I haven't seen him ever since the morning he was yelling at Mama June. Mama June is at work and Grandma Gin is out of town for a doctor's appointment. I had the house all to myself... which gave me the chance to search John's room. I rifle through his stuff searching for anything that could point in the direction of where he was when he was away for five months. I look in his drawers, closet, desk and under the bed, but I couldn't find anything. Until I remembered a movie, and in this movie, the bad guy hides a safe behind a picture. But John didn't have any pictures, instead, he has a few posters. I look behind one poster of a spaceship, then another of a cat with glasses, then the last one of a treasure chest, and that's when I saw it, a safe.

Chapter 6

The Safe

I'm staring at the safe, thinking of what could be in there. Passports, money, and the picture? I must get into that safe. I placed the poster back on the wall then immediately went to the internet to research, how to crack a safe. By the time I thought I had it figured out, John walked in.

"We need to talk." His face is stern.

"Yes, we do." My voice seeping with cold.

"So when did you see the man?"

"Last night. Who is he?"

"He's our cousin, and he's very dangerous. So I need you to tell me every everything." John's reached out his hands grabbing mine. His eyes are full of concern.

"Okay, but how is he dangerous?"

"That's not important right now, what is important is that you tell me what he looked like and if he talked to you."

"It is important, and he looked exactly like how he looked in the picture."

"Thank you." John hugged me then left.

"Wait!" I yell after him, but yet again he's gone. I returned to my room. How could I have a cousin? Uncle Larry was Mama June's only brother, and as long as I could remember Uncle Larry has always been here, I thought, or has he? I was thinking when I saw a text come through my phone.

'Hey, princess.' Luke insist on calling me princess ever since the night at the fair.

'Hey, pretty boy.' I typed. Knowing he wouldn't like it.

'What are you up to?'

'I'm trying something.'

'What is it, maybe I can help?'

'Do you know how to crack a safe?'

'Yes, but if you're planning on robbing a bank, I'll have to report you.'

'Ha Ha Ha you're very funny.' I smiled as I typed.

'I know, so whose safe needs cracking.' As I read the text I thought, I shouldn't get him involved, as John stated, it's dangerous.

'It was a joke. I'm actually doing nothing right now.' I typed, I thought of using him just for this one thing but, I knew it would kill me if anyone got in trouble.

'Hmm okay, do you want to hang out with Kim, Madison, and me at the pier tomorrow?'

'Sure.' Hanging out with my friends should help remove the idea that my family is in danger. Why would he want to hurt us? I wondered as I sat on my bed. I began to see why John was being reserved, yet I still think that there's something more to John's trip and this cousin. I need to crack that safe.

I marched over to John's room, taking the poster off the wall to reveal the silver square with a circular dial, that has numbers ranging from zero to fifty on it. As I recall the video about safecracking, I heard loud footsteps approaching. Panic stirred in my eyes as I look around the room for a place to hide. I run into the closet and shut the door securing it with a wire clothes hanger. I untwisted it and threaded it through the slits and back towards me then twisting the wire again so that the doors are secured. The footsteps entered the room just as I twisted the wire. Then, I realized I left the safe exposed.

"Boss there it is." A high-pitched voice spoke with a hint of nervousness.

"What are you waiting for? Get it open." The man they called the boss has a thick British accent. Through the slits, I saw a scrawny red-haired boy and two bulky men, and between them a tall man. His skin was a pasty white, and he wears a black suit that looks Italian. He has a ring on the pinky finger of the right hand. The ring is gold with a bear on it, which reminded me of a news article that talked about the Italian Mafia and their symbols. Tears started to roll down my face; my heart starts to beat faster which I thought was impossible until now. I have an overwhelming urge to scream for help, but I know that would just get me into more danger.

"We got it, boss." The red-haired boy said. I adjusted my view to try and see what they were taking, but I couldn't get a good look.

"Let's go." The boss snapped, and, just like that, they were gone. I started to cry harder as I undid my makeshift lock. Soon the tears were uncontrollable, I slumped down to the closet's floor. Crying into my hands.

Once I ran out of tears, I finished undoing the clothes hanger. I stumbled over to the open safe to see that it's empty. I turned around, and a shimmer of light caught my eye. I slowly turn towards the safe and see a clip on the inside. I fiddled with it until it released a trap door. That's when I saw it, a file, labeled confidential with a government seal in the corner that read CIA, Central Intelligence Agency. I slowly reached in and grabbing the thick vanilla folder I saw a name on the tab that read, John C. Carmichael.

My brother is CIA.

I stood in shock as I read the name over and over again. How? When? How long had John been lying to us? This revelation brought chills, I didn't know what to do. I debated to put it back as if I never saw it, or I could take the file and read it. I decided to look over it before I would place it back.

In the file, there's multiple redacted papers with pictures of surveillance footage of what looks to be like John. The time stamp read 10/30/14, that was two years ago when John said he was at a writing seminar for his college classes. How long has he been with the CIA? There are multiple other dates more recent, too, as far back as four years ago. As I continue to search for clues to who the man is from the Italian Mafia, I found a redacted document that could possibly lead to the answer. It's only a few pieces, but it had enough to form the conclusion that the government had John steal from the Italians, as an effort to stop their empire from expanding. Obviously, it failed, and now my family is paying for it.

I'm lying in bed thinking of my new realization about my family and how I had to go out tomorrow and pretend that nothing happened to keep my friends safe. My stomach turns at the thought of the possibility of my friends getting hurt. That night I locked my door and squeezed my eyes shut.

Chapter 7

The Beginning

My hands are secured to a wooden chair, three men are surrounding me. I try to cry but no sound comes out. The men approach me with a knife.

I wake up to my hands shaking and my clothes soaked with sweat. It was just a bad dream I keep reminding myself. I slowly got out of bed and start towards the shower in hope of washing away the nightmare and to get ready to meet up with Kim, Madison, and Luke.

The warmth of the water and the light of the day brings a comfort, after what happened last night. The memory of those men, and of John made it all surreal to me. The fact that sweet John is a cold-hearted spy and has been lying to me ever since, well forever. Now because of that, my family is in danger. Mama June and Grandma Gin should've been worried about John's job, not Uncle Larry's. This runs through my mind as I got dressed. I put on light-color, acid-washed jean shorts paired with a white top that shows my tone stomach from the years of Systema, Russian martial arts that focus on close quarters combat and disarming along with parkour. My brother John suggested the classes and took them with me, I use to think it was a bonding moment but now I'm convinced it was just for work. I shook my head trying to focus on my clothes again and look at my outfit. Then decide to put on a red flannel to balance out the absence of color with color. And for my shoes, my favorite pair of converses. I look over my outfit, then headed out the door.

When I arrive, the sky is gloomy with clouds, and the air is still. Seagulls fly overhead, and the soothing sound of the rough bay, made it a beautiful day. Luke is sitting on a bench and beside him, Kim and Madison. Madison waved me over.

"Hey," I said with a smile.

"Hey," Kim said, Madison and Luke followed suit.

"What do we want to do?" I said. Kim stood up beside me, while Luke and Madison stayed on the bench.

"How about we go for some coffee, then to the mall? Luke said.

"Sounds like a plan," Kim said. I nod my head in agreement.

"Sweet let's go," Madison said as she grabs Luke's arm pulling him towards the Coffee House. I stay back with Kim.

"So is John home?" Kim said with a smile, but as soon as I heard his name, I became fused with anger.

"I don't know, John left last night." The words coming out of my mouth made me realize, that John never returned home. Where could he be?

"Jacy? Jacy? Hello?" Kim nudged me as we are walking.

"Hey, sorry my mind kind of wandered off." I shook my head as though it would bring me back to earth, to the conversation, to normal life.

"We're here." Kim smiles and took the seat across from Madison. So that left only one seat open.

"Hmm does anyone want anything to drink?" I said in an effort to prolong the uncomfortable PDA trying to be displayed by Madison and Luke.

"I'm good for now thank you though." Kim gave me a reassuring smile.

"I'm also good," Madison said as she leans closer to Luke, who then stands up.

"I'll come with you. Drinks are on me." His voice is rushed. I could tell he's uncomfortable with Madison hanging on him.

"Okay, let's go." I turn on my heels and start towards the register.

"So, did you ever get into that safe?" Luke whispers into my ear. My face got hot, as he started to grin.

"Yes." My voice is short for I wasn't in the mood for his games.

"What did you find?"

"Nothing of importance to you," I said as we reach the counter.

"I want a black coffee, and whatever the lady wants," Luke smirks and, gives me a subtle wink. I roll my eyes as I look at the menu.

"I'll have a caramel mocha and a bagel, please." I smile.

"That will be fifteen ninety-nine, Sir." I snicker at the sound of someone calling Luke Sir. Luke looks at me and starts to move closer, I back up into a shelf. His eyes are an ocean blue that give away a hint of desire. I couldn't look away no matter how much I want to I was locked.

"Like what you see?" Luke throws me a flirtatious smile.

"Nope." I throw him a seductive look.

"Here's your coffees Sir." And just like that, the moment was over.

"Thank you." I grab my coffee and immediately start back to the table where Kim and Madison are having an intense talk about how many shoes are too many. I avoid eye contact with Luke and Madison for the rest of our afternoon. By the time we got done with our coffee, I decided it was time for me to go home, no matter how much I would come to dread it.

Once I got home, to see John sitting on the steps. What could he want? The man is putting my family in danger, and he just sits there. All my anger came to the top as I approach him.

"What do you want?" I stand three feet away, a safe distance according to my training.

"I need to relocate you to a safe house. Mama June and Josh are there." His voice cracked with remorse. He already knew what I would say.

"No." I take a defensive position as he stands up.

"Come on Jacy, it's not safe here anymore." His arms are stretched out in a pleading manner.

"And whose fault is that?" My eyes start to swell up.

"I know." His eyes are red for a moment then they return to normal.

I shake my head in disgust. "No, I'm staying here."

"You won't survive." He snaps.

"I guess we'll see." I turn away from John and walk to my car then drove off. Oh, we'll see. I thought we'll see.

Chapter 8

Captured

I've been driving around for hours; I don't know where I'm going or what I'm going to do. My family is gone. I have nowhere to go. Where do I go from here? I park my car and start to walk. The evening is cold and the smell of the salt off the bay reminds me of John. When we were younger, John and I would go snorkeling and scuba diving along the bay and out into the Pacific Ocean. A smile grew as tears rolled down my face, I start to laugh hysterically. The memory is amusing, for he wasn't really there as my brother. I walk till I reach a bridge. How much danger can I possibly be in?

I look out towards the bay; a boat sits just off the coast. The sailboat has two main masts and what looks like a house in the haul as well. I see two men on the boat. It's too dark to make out their description but one of the men is holding something. I stare for a while thinking of what it could be when a glimpse of light catches my eye, a reflection of the moon off the glass, it's a scope.

I duck and move behind a car when a shot rang throughout the air. I need to call someone, but who, Luke Reynolds. He's the only one I would gladly risk his life for. I start to dial three-three-five, when a car comes screeching around the corner. My eyes stretch wide, and my brain froze. What do I do now? The car is advancing fast, my heart drops as I think what to do. Run, I turn on my heels and sprint towards the nearest alley I can barely fit through it. I use momentum while I spring off one wall to a ledge. Four men got out of the car, two young redheaded boys around my age climb after me, while the other two got back in the car and start to pursue me from the ground. I reach the roof and bolt towards a door, lock then another, lock. This is a fire hazard I thought, I suddenly stop at a gap. It's about an eighty-foot drop. I look back to see the two boys are closing in. I turn around run a few steps then face the gap. My breath is shallow as I take a deep breath in and run, three, two, one. I leap over the ravine. Everything appears to be moving in slow motion. A jolt of pain travels from the point of impact to my head. My vision blurs, and a piercing pain in my side brings tears to my eyes. I must have broken a rib or two. I grimace when I try to lift myself from the rooftop. I glance back at the two boys who are staring at me from across the building that I had just leaped from.

"Who are you?" I command.

"You'll learn soon enough who we are." The bigger boy spoke. The other boy looks at him in disappointment and drags him away. I sink to my knees. Suddenly my sight began to disappear, while the increasing pain became intolerable. My body collapsed, and everything went dark.

The sound of clinking pipes and water dripping make my headache spread and my eyesight blur. There are lights shining lights amidst men with masks enclosing me.

"She's waking up. Deliver her another dose." Says the man with glasses with a headlamp attached, his eyes are a gold, and his mouth is covered by a blue mask. My eyes trace the room, it looks like a cargo pit, of a plane. Where am I? I try to sit up but straps prevent me. I thrash in panic.

"Put her out," A bold voice says. I can't see who it is. My eyes got heavy as I slip into a state of sleep.

It's cold for the middle of summer, my eyes slowly open. My head is pounding from the pain in my side. I reach towards the wound and wince as I sit up. I scan the room for any details to where I could be. The bed is covered with a heavy white comforter, an animal skin rug is placed by a fireplace that isn't doing its job. I'm wearing a tight black tank-top with black military cargo pants. My socks feel like wool, and over by the fireplace are black combat boots and a coat. My head pounds, I bite my lip in pain when I stand out of bed.

"Well good morning princess." Only one man ever called me that, Luke Reynolds. I must have called him before I passed out. I turn towards him. Luke has on a heavy black coat with military cargo pants and boots. I walk over to him, and without thinking wrap my arms around him. I couldn't hold it back anymore, tears pour down my face, partly for the pain and partly is the feeling of finally having someone I can trust.

"Where am I?" I pull away just enough to look into his eyes.

"We are in Russia," he smiles, "put on your shoes and follow me."

There's no way I can be in Russia, it feels as though I was only out for a couple of hours. How could I be in Russia? I walk over to my boots and place them on each foot. I tie a basic square loop knot that my brother taught me during our adventure in the European Alps. I stand up slowly and start towards the door where Luke had exited. A frigid wind hits me as I walk out the door. Luke looks over his shoulder at me and smiles.

"What took you so long?" He laughs.

"Oh, I don't know, probably the unbearable pain in my side." I roll my eyes.

"The doctors said they wrapped it," he looks concern, "I'll talk to them later."

"Are you going to tell me what happened, and why I'm here?"

"Yes, all in due time." He smiles and walks into a tent.

No now, I thought, but reluctantly I followed him into the tent. Realizing that I can't get any answers if I didn't go with him. The tent is huge and filled with rows of tables like my cafeteria back home. There are men and woman chowing down on what I would call frozen oatmeal. Luke walks right past the line and into a private room. The air is warm, and a plate of ham is in the center of the table with a bowl of salad and a glass of wine. Luke sit on one side of the table and me on the other.

"Would you like for me to carve you a piece of ham? Or do you want to do it yourself?" Luke possesses a certain politeness and an authority.

"What I would like is for you to tell me what the hell is going on!" I snap, which I regret. With every breath I take, the pain increased. I attempt to hide it, but Luke saw my face as it contorted with pain.

"I will but you need to eat to keep up your strength." Luke takes a piece of ham.

"I don't want to eat." My breath becomes quick, and my head felt as if it was floating. I'm on the verge of passing out. "I want to know why I'm here." I said breathless.

"Okay but let me look at your wound first." His smile is, kind, as he walks towards me. I'm too weak to protest. I lift the side of my shirt, exposing a pink wrap, secured tightly around my ribs. Luke gently unwraps it to reveal a gash along with four stitches. His hand skims my side sending a surge of pain throughout my body. I jerk back, biting my lip to keep me from screaming. "Sorry." He smells like a fresh breath of a winter's first snowfall. He looks up at me, we are breathing the same air, he starts to lean in. My body on fire with an uncontrollable attraction, I know I shouldn't act on it. No matter how much I want to. I repeat to myself, self-control Jacy, self-control.

"What are you doing?" I whisper as my urge to give in increased.

Luke's eyes search mine. "What are you doing?"

"I," my voice low, "I think this is my chair." Luke smirks and slowly backs away. Then return to his seat with confident smile. "Now, can you tell me what I'm doing in Russia?" I say with my face still hot.

"Yes, what's the last thing you remember." Luke's voice is calm and soothing.

"I remember landing on a roof and pain."

"Okay, so I'm involved with some people, and I heard you were in trouble. I put in a few words and now you're here." Luke put his hands out to the side then laces them back together.

"Who are you involved with? And there's more to the story, tell me everything."

"Now that's need to know, and you don't need to know." A thoughtful smile appears.

"Oh, and you see when I arrived at the rooftop, I saw you crumpled on the ground, your head was bleeding as were your arm where you scrapped it on the rooftop. I gave you a sedative to keep you asleep while we fixed you up and transported you to Russia." His smile is reassuring.

"But why?"

"Why what?"

"Why Russia?"

"Well you see, my people agreed that Russia would be the safest place for you."

"Wait, your people? And do you know who was chasing me?" I reached for a slice of ham. Luke saw me struggle and brought me a piece.

"Yes and no. Yes, my people and no, I don't but I'm looking into it." Luke said as I began to nod off. "Hey, I think this is a little too much how about you go to bed and heal."

"No, I'm fine." I wave him off as I take a bite of ham.

"No, you're not let's go," Luke came over and picked me up. I wrap my arms around his neck and lay my head on his chest, the soothing sound of his breathing and his muscles lifting his chest up and down.

"I was fine, you know." He sets me down gently and covers me up with the fluffy white comforter and kisses my forehead. I'm delusional at that point. I didn't know whether it's a dream or reality.

"I know princess, I know." Everything went black as Luke walks out the door.

Chapter 9

Russian Camp

I'm running through a dense forest, I don't know how many there are, or who is after me. I leap over a log then duck under another. I see a figure approaching me from the front, I turn right, I can feel my heart beat in my ears. Another figure is running at me, I turn around to face a man, I try to run past him but, I can't move. My arms are being held behind me. The man raises a gun to my head.

"Jacy, Jacy. It's time for you to get up we have a big day today," I jump, my eyes widen with terror. "Jacy, are you okay?" Luke gently moves my hair behind my ears.

"Yeah, just a nightmare." I smile, and my eyes wander towards the door where two men dressed in black stood with holstered pistols and automatic weapons slung across their bodies.

"Hey, don't worry. I'm here." Luke smiles and reaches his hand out in an offer to help me stand up. I would have taken it, but I want to prove that I'm not weak. Especially after last night. He bows his head and shakes with laughter. I bit my lip when I try to stand up to keep me from screaming in pain.

"Your clothes are on the chair, call me when you're done getting dressed. We have a lot of stuff to do today." Luke speaks with an authority that's reflects in his stance. His shoulders back, chin up, his hands were behind his back or in his pockets. His smile is gentle and polite. Luke snaps his fingers, and the men exit with him. I limp over to my pile of clothes. Luke obviously didn't have fashion sense. It's the same outfit as yesterday. All black militia outfit. I put on each item, and out of the corner of my eye I watch the door, in an effort to make sure no one could attack me. I jump when I hear a knock at the door.

"Miss Jacy? Mr. Reynolds would like you to come to the dining hall once you are done getting dressed." A man's voice said.

"Okay, I'll be there in a second," I yell. I finish tying my shoes, and slowly make my way to the dining hall. The snow's floating down, men huddle around barrels with smoke floating out of them. My eyes scan the landscape, nothing looks the same as last night. Of course, I'm delusional from the drug Luke gave me. Yet, I can still vividly remember eating with Luke and his hand skimming my side in an attempt to make sure my wound was healing. Luke must have wrapped my side or had one of his minions do it. My arm rests across my body. I walk into the dining hall and see Luke at the end of the room. His dirty blond hair is perfectly combed back, and his face brightens when he waves me over. I try to push through the men when a guy stops me. He is tall and bulky with a thick beard and bushy eyebrows. I look up at him and attempt to maneuver around him, but he steps in front of me.

"Excuse me," I say politely. He belches out a laugh.

"No, but you can come to my room you pretty little thing." He reaches out to grab me, I evade his hands and attempt to kick out his legs. He stands up straight, turns towards me and growls. *Oh, no*, is the only thought that went through my mind, before he swiftly kicked me in the side. My eyes started to swell, as the pain travels throughout my body. The burly man tries another kick but this time I duck and sweep his leg to throw him off balance. This gives me enough time to turn towards Luke, who isn't there anymore. I frantically search for his face. I feel a hand on my shoulder, I grab it with my opposite hand and duck under then twists his arm.

"Enough!" Luke's voice rang through the tent. The man dropped to his knees. I kept my hold of his arm, "Jacy, let go of his arm." Luke's voice is low and authoritative, his blue eyes meet mine, his hand outstretched. I loosen my grip slowly, the corners of my eyes are fuzzy from the pain in my side. I stumbled towards Luke. He pulls me into a hug.

"Help," I whispers, I try to suck in my tears.

"I got you. Don't worry I got you." Luke's breath is warm, "I'm going to have one of my men take you to the room we were in last night. Okay?" His voice is reassuring.

"Okay." I step away from Luke as one of his men showed me the way. I feel stupid realizing how weak I am. I lift my shirt to reveal bandages, and I unwrap my side. Blood is trickling down my side. I take a breath and start to re-wrap my wound. I was protecting myself, I told myself when I heard a scream. I look at guard then look away. I wish my family was here with me. I smile at the thought of a family dinner with John and Josh, Grandma Gin and Uncle Larry. Back when all I had to worry about was if it was my week for chores.

"So, we are going on a trip," Luke said as he walks in the door and signals for his men to leave.

"Where?" I said, with a painful grin.

"London, actually just outside of London."

"Hmm, what for? And do I get an option in this matter?" My voice is filled with annoyance.

"You'll find out when we get there and sadly no."

"Why not?"

"Because I need to know you're safe, and considering the events that happened today, I think it would be best if you stick next to me." Luke smiles confidently.

I take an offense to this. I purse my lips and roll my eyes. "I can protect myself thank you very much," I said picking at the tablecloth.

"I don't doubt that," Luke smiles and makes his way to the seat beside me, "But still I would feel better if you were next to me."

"Why London?"

"Because my boss has a job for you."

"What's the job?"

"You'll find out when you get there." Luke smiles, "Let's eat."

"What did you do with that man?" I said, my voice has a trace of fear in it. Luke looks at my eyes, trying to decide what to say.

"I took care of it."

"What did you do?"

"I moved him to a different post." His eyes are distant in a way. He's lying. Luke leans in, his ocean eyes never shift from mine, pondering if he should speak or not, "let's eat." What was he going to say? Luke has something he wants to share, some emotion that he's been trying to withhold from me. Could it be if he shows emotion the world would end? I snicker at this thought. Men... always hiding their true feelings.

After I eat, Luke's men escort me back to my tent where a cup, towel and a bowl of warm water are on the little table by the fireplace. I make my way over and take a cup and fill it full of water. How am I going to do this? I thought for five minutes then began to pour the water over my head. Once I finish, I put my hair up in a ponytail. My long dirty blond hair reaches between my shoulder blades. As I finish getting ready for what Luke calls a 'road trip,' I start thinking of my family, and friends. I should have gone to the safe house with John. I shake my head in disappointment in myself. Why did I have to be so stubborn? My eyes start to fill with water, I quickly wipe them away as Luke enters the room.

"You ready?" Luke said. Was I ready? I didn't know, but what I did know is that I didn't have a choice.

Chapter 10

Training

We are in a green truck; Luke and I are in the back. It's snowing outside as we move along the countryside. My eyes keep drifting towards Luke whose eyes seem to do the same. Every once in a while, we hit a rock or a pothole that would jolt my body up against the door, and I let out a low growl, my side is still bruised black and blue from the fight yesterday, and from jumping onto another building. I've been on this truck for twelve hours now. My stomach is starting to grumble for food.

"When are we stopping?" I ask Luke. He looks at his watch then at the road.

"In about ten minutes. We'll eat, and I will show you some combat moves you will need when we arrive in London."

"You are going to teach me how to fight?" My voice irritated, I just kicked a man's ass that's twice my size and pretty boy Luke wants to train me.

"Yes, my employer would like you to be prepared when we get to London. So every few hours we will stop and train. Unless you're still hurt..." Luke gestures towards my side where my hand covers the wound.

"No, I'm ready. Are you?" I lift an eyebrow to challenge him.

"Yes." Luke laughs and moves closer to me, and whispers, "Just one thing."

"What?" My cheeks grow hot.

"Don't get distracted by my looks."

I rolled my eyes. "Impossible, but I wish you luck because there's no way you can resist me," I smirk. Luke looks me up and down with a shoulder shrug.

"I have self-control. You don't," before I could slap him with a comeback, the truck stops. I step outside of the truck to see a small building with a sign that's weathered away. This is where we're stopping? My face contorts with confusion.

"Follow me, princess." Luke grabs my hand pulling me towards the door. His hands are callused. I feel a sense of security with my hand in his. My face flush with red, a small smile grew on my face. Luke leads me to a shelf stocked with cans of soup, and cereal boxes. I look at Luke as he reaches out and pressed a button under the shelf then gave me a smile when a door appears to the right of us.

"Is that supposed to impress me?" I throw him a flirtatious smile.

"No, but what's behind the door will." Luke nudges me and pulls me towards the door. We make our way down the stairs, that lead us to a huge room with a kitchen. It has four different hallways leading to other rooms.

"Woah, what is this place?" My eyes wander around the room.

"It's called The House. We use it when we need to hide out, restock, or rest. But tonight, we are using it to train you."

"Okay, so what room are we going to train in?" I laugh at the word train, little did he acknowledge I know how to fight.

"Right this way." Luke did a semi-bow towards the main hallway. The bright fluorescent lights make the white walls seem brighter, as we make our way to the very end room. The room is bare. I stand in the center of the room scanning, memorizing every detail. In the corner of the room, I spot a poster: with a lion with a pair of swords behind its head. There are words at the base of the poster, 'The Front'.

"What's The Front?" I ask.

"It's the organization that I work for." Luke smile, "now let's begin."

I look at Luke with a daring smile. "Okay, come at me."

"First let's go over a few steps." Luke talks about basic hold and evasion, while he shows me. "Now attack me."

I take a few steps forward and throw a punch, Luke dodges with speed, while swiping my legs out from under me. I flip up and smiled.

"Smooth." I'm surprised that Luke actually got the best of me.

"Keep your elbows up and your feet shoulder width apart." Luke pounces. I slip through his arms and kick him in the back.

"Keep up." I smile, he shakes his head as he throws a punch and kicks me in the side. I collapse from the pain. I can't show weakness I thought, as I sweep his legs out. He lands on his back, I jump on him and place his hands above his head.

"Not too bad," His smile seductive and his eyes enchanting, My face ruby red.

"I won." I smile, we sat in this position. The pain in my side grew when my adrenaline settled down. Luke's eyes grew concern as pain appeared on my face.

"Jacy, are you alright?" My hands slip from his, my vision starts to blur. Luke slowly migrates to a sitting position.

"I'm fine." I shake my head; my vision went in and out. Luke's arms wrap around me when I fell into his chest, "I'm fine."

"No, you're not. Let me help you." His voice is kind, his hands gentle as he moves my hair behind my ears. We are so close that we are sharing every breath.

"I'm fine, Luke. Honest." When I look into his eyes, they're filled with passion. Luke's lips hit mine with a gentle kiss then began to change as we fought with a hunger. I crave him, Luke's hand lightly moves under my shirt gradually to the small of my back while his other is drawing my face down towards his. The air sucked out of my lungs, my heart is pounding in my ears, I work my fingers through his hair. Luke abruptly tore away, leaving his lip like a ghost on mine.

"We shouldn't be doing this, sorry," Luke said breathless, but his eyes said another.

"Why?" I tilt my head in confusion.

"It's complicated," his head sunk, he looks at me with a fire still in his eyes, he bit his lip, "we should go."

"I guess so..." My voice trails off. Luke stands up and offers me a hand. I ignore it pulling myself up off the cold floor. Thinking, *What just happened?*

***

It's been a few days since Jacy was taken, and John looked everywhere for her. John's contacts got him in touch with a man who pointed him to the bay area. Where he found her car. There was no trace of a struggle in the car. This led him to assume she was walking or somewhere else when she was taken. John walked around showing a picture of Jacy, he also asked building managers for tapes. That's when he found Jacy running from two men on the roof. And he saw a man he wished he didn't, his cousin.

John walked into the safe house to see Josh and Mama June sitting at the table. He had a bag with him. He placed the bag on the table.

"Mama June, Josh. I have to go find Jacy. She's been taken by this man." John reached into his pocket and pulled out a picture.

"Who is he?" Josh asked.

"His name is Gabriel he's our cousin. A few weeks ago he showed up. Gabriel has had it out for me ever since I went away."

"How did he know about Jacy?" Mama June asked. John's eyes were filled with guilt.

"Me," John said.

"I knew it. Ever since you joined the agency, Jacy would be in danger." Josh pointed his finger at John.

"Hey, I knew my job came with a risk so I took measures to make sure Jacy would be okay. I trained her, and now that I found out who took her, I'm going to go get her." John's voice was filled with determination.

"It's no one's fault." Mama June's eyes began to fill with tears. Josh walked over and hugged her.

"Everything will be alright. John will fix this mess. Right?" Josh whispered and looked at John.

"Yes, I will. Jacy will be safe before you know it." John grabbed his bag including the gun on the bar, then vanished behind the door.

Chapter 11

London

One, two, three, four, bang. A shot rings throughout the bunker. Luke steps behind me, I grow stiff when his hand touches my shoulder and abdomen.

"Keep your arms firm, and your abs tight." Luke utters softly, "and don't forget to breathe." I try to shake the image of Luke's lips brushing mine out of my mind. The idea of us is absurd, I fire another shot. He's keeping things from me, and he kidnapped me. Now he's taking me to his boss, and Luke won't tell me who his boss is. Plus how did he have the connections to bring me to Russia. He's not trustworthy, and I don't know anything about him. Is his name really Luke? I fire my last round, then place the gun on the table. Luke beckons to me, which I overlook, and instead march over to the table with the bullets and the rest of the guns. I fiddle with the bullets filling the clip, half hoping for Luke to approach me.

"Jacy, time to go." Luke's' voice traveled through the bunker. I mimic Luke and start to pack up. I hear the door close behind me. They left me to pack up everything. I glance at the bags then at the door. If they don't have to carry anything, then I shouldn't either and I walked out the door. Luke's eyes seem brighter in the sunlight. I try to avoid eye contact. "Jacy, can we talk?"

"Sorry, we can't," I attempt to walk past him, he grasps my elbow.

"Come now." He whispers with a stern voice while pulling me behind the truck.

"Let go of me." I yank my arm away, "Who do you think you are!" He places his finger on my lips.

"Shhh. They can't know. If they know, it could get us killed." His eyes fill with fear.

"If who knows and if they know what?" I take a step closer.

"About us." He tilted his head slightly, "My boss will kill us."

"What do you mean? Why?"

"Because I'm not supposed to get involved with you." His hands rub the side of my arms.

"Okay, well you're safe then because there isn't an us." I start to turn away. He grabs my arm firmly; my face contorts with pain. Luke notices and releases my arm.

"Sorry, but there is an us. You can't tell me you felt nothing when we kissed." His eyes grew sad as if I already answer.

"I... Don't... Know. It doesn't matter. As you said it's complicated." My eyes trace his for a sense of hope. Instead, I found sadness.

"Mr. Luke, you ready?" One of his men say. Luke searches my face.

"Hmm yes, we are ready. Let's load up." Luke returns to his polite personality. Luke reaches around me, and opens the door, "after you, princess." I furrow my eyebrows.

"Don't call me princess," I say as I jump in the truck.

"Whatever you say, princess." His lips curls upwards revealing perfect white teeth as he winks. Luke gives his men orders to go down and grab the guns, while he fuels up the truck. We are about a hundred miles from Berlin, and it has been a total of five days and three hours since I've arrived in Russia. I miss my family, the game nights where my brothers and I would gang up on Mama June and Grandma Gin. I wonder if they even know I'm gone. It doesn't matter anyway, I'm safer here than back home, where I'm being chased by men with guns. Who do they work for? The red-headed boys knew or had some training to be able to climb after me. They used a technique that I've only seen John use during one of our adventures in the Alps. We had a race to see who can get from point A to point B the fastest using only a map and a knife. When he ran, he would leap from one log onto another while pushing his body weight forward. John always told me that it helped you to be light on your feet, you move faster and smoother, this draws less attention to you. Tears began to surface at the thought of my family. I quickly blink them away. Don't show weakness, not here, not now. I look out the window to see Luke's men rushing over to him. The men pull Luke away from the car, I couldn't make out what they were saying, but it made Luke mad. The men shake their heads in agreement.

"I've got some bad news," Luke said as he jumps in the car.

"Yes?" My voice intrigued.

"We won't be able to eat until twenty-one hundred hours tonight." Luke forged a smile. There's something he's not telling me. Is it because his men would tell his boss?

"Okay, is there anything else?" I try to pry for something more, for the truth.

"Nope." Luke smiles.

I slump back in my seat. What did his men say? Luke's hand slides behind my back. I jolt upwards, "what are you doing?" I whisper harshly, slightly confused after what he just said outside of the truck.

"Sorry, I left my pen on the seat, and it migrated behind your back." Luke pulls a pen out and smiles knowing that I thought something different.

"Oh, it's fine," I turn my face away from Luke hoping that he didn't catch how embarrassed I am. I feel his eyes resting on me, and his confident smile burning a hole in my chest, He saw.

***

It's 19:00 when John arrives in London. He is met by his handler. They are heading toward their base outside of London.

"Are you sure you want to do this? It could compromise your mission and your place in the agency." The handler is classically handsome with a black suit and his black hair slicked back.

"Yes, I need to get my sister back. It's my fault she was taken. I got her into this mess, I have to get her out of this before." John's eyes wander off.

"You're too involved. You can't do this." His handler pulls out his phone.

"Who are you calling?" John's face stern, his eyes cold.

"I'm calling a friend at the SIS."

"No, I can do this. We don't need to involve them." John knew if they involved the Secret Intelligence Service they wouldn't understand how important Jacy is, or they will discover who she's involved with and use her. John couldn't let that happen. She's not ready for a mission. On the other hand, *I could compromise my identity and she could get killed.* John sighed in frustration.

"We have to. I can't help you compromise yourself and I know they will help her." His handler assures him.

"No, it's safer if I just bring her home." John raises his voice.

"No, I'm calling them. You will sit and watch while I help bring Jacy home. You can be the guy behind the mic. Heard but not seen. You can be in control of the operation." John thought about it, he replays his options in mind. Compromise himself but bring Jacy home, or hand over Jacy's life to the SIS, but have limited control over the operation. Either option could result in Jacy getting hurt.

"I will have control over the operation?"

"Yes."

"Okay, make it happen, but if something goes wrong. I'm stepping in."

"Driver to SIS headquarters."

"Yes, Sir." The driver said.

John looks out the window, he thought back to the five months he was undercover. His mission to take down The Front. John thought of when he first met Gabriel, it was when he finished his first introduction to The Front. John's stomach turns at the memory of what he did. John clenches his jaw to keep screaming in anger. Gabriel will pay if he hurts her. The thought of Gabriel's dark brown eyes even looking at Jacy or his blood-stained hands getting close to her.

"After Jacy is safe, I'll find Gabriel and Kill him." John whispers in a voice low.

"You want to go back in?"

"Yes, once my sister is safe. I'll go back in."

"Good decision, John." His handler grabbed two glasses and a bottle of whiskey. He poured a skim of whiskey in each glass, "to Project Maverick."

John threw the glass back, and with one gulp, it vanished.

"Get me their best agent."

"I already have an agent in mind."

"Who?" John's voice filled with doubt.

"He's around Jacy's age, and before you say he's too young, just trust me you want him."

John nods his head knowing that a kid would be less conspicuous especially since he has to infiltrate The Front.

"Okay, but I want to meet with him before I put my sister's life in his arms."

"You are about to, we're here." John looks out the window as they pull up to an elegant building. The building was six stories with a training facility to the left. It was magnificent the glass reflecting the sun made a halo around the building. John is greeted at the door with a tall sliver haired man.

"Hello Mr. Carmichael, follow me please." The man has a thick British accent. John follows the man into the building, down two corridors and into an office that looks out towards the training facility. "He will be right in Mr. Carmichael."

"Thank you," John said as the man left the room. John has on black slacks and a blue collared long sleeve shirt and a black suit coat that hid the gun resting in a holster on his rib cage.

"John, right?" A man walks in with a blue suit on and a case file in his right hand.

"Yes," John answered, "who are you?"

"I'm the director of the SIS. My name is James Carter, how may I help you?"

"My sister has been taken by The Front, they are a dangerous organization. I need your help getting my sister back before I began Project Maverick again." John hands the case file on Project Maverick over.

"I'll read this then decide if we will help you." James grabs the file, "I'll be in contact." John retraces his steps back to the car.

"How did it go?" John's handler spoke in a concerned voice.

"Good, let's go to the base and set up." John gave the driver a nod to drive, "James will be calling shortly."

Chapter 12

The Man

When I was a kid John would bring me snow globes after every trip. The first one that I got had skyscrapers around a park, and at the bottom of the globe was the words 'New York'. I loved getting them. They always made me feel a part of his trips and I knew he was thinking of me when he was gone. As the land rolled by, I wished it was a snow globe. I wish that this is all a dream and that I could wake up knowing my family is safe and that I'm safe. I wonder what my family is doing? I know John has them in a safe house; where they're probably watching Tv, not realizing that I'm gone. Knowing I made my decision, Luke touches my hand, my body tingles at his warmth. I hate that I like it, I slid my hand away.

"Jacy, we are just outside of Belgium."

"Okay, so we will be stopping soon?"

"Yes, so start preparing yourself," Luke said, his smile concerned. I tilt my head. Something is wrong.

"Prepare for what?"

"I'll brief you when we arrive." Luke reaches behind his back, "here you'll need this." Luke pulls out a Glock, I shake my head.

"No, why would I need that?" The thought of having to kill someone makes my heart drop.

"Don't worry, it's just for protection. Only use it if you have to." His voice is reassuring. The cold metal feels heavy in my hand, even though I spent the last two stops learning disarming techniques and how to fire and load a gun.

"What am I going to do?"

"I'll tell you once we arrive." Luke lays his hand on my shoulder as if he could comfort me. As soon as he sees my reaction, he takes his hand away and smiles, "It'll be fine, I'll be there the whole time." That isn't comforting.

"Okay, I trust you." I smile, as I place my hand on his knee. I lean into him, "I'm going to find out anyway, so you might as well tell me." I whisper seductively into his ear. His blue eyes sparkle with passion. Then he grins, realizing what I'm trying to do.

"I could, but you'll have to do something for me," Luke whispers back, knowing that if his men find out they would tell his boss.

"And that is?" I drew closer.

"Kiss me again." Luke whispers seductively.

I tilt my head from side to side, considering it. "Okay, deal. Now tell me."

Luke smiles. "You are going to a dinner to watch this man." Luke pulls a picture from his pocket. The man is classically handsome, he looks to be around fifty years old.

"Who is he?"

"That's not important, but what is, is that you follow him." Luke hands me a pair of glasses and an earpiece, "wear these glasses, they have a camera, so I'll be able to see what you're seeing, also put this in. This is how I will be able to talk to you."

"Okay, what am I going to wear?" Luke smiles.

"I have a dress for you, we will stop at a hotel where you will change and get ready for the dinner." Luke looks me up and down, "Also don't get caught."

We pull over at a hotel, Luke told me that the dinner starts at nineteen hundred hours. I only have an hour to get ready and figure out why they need me to follow this man. Luke lead me to a room. The room has a single queen bed with a

Tv, and an elegant dresser, the wallpaper is a striped gold and a cream white.

"So what's this dinner about? So if I am talking, I know what to talk about."

"It's a charity, and that's all you need to know." Luke shuts the door as he makes his way over to me with a dress, "here. Go change."

"It's beautiful." The dress is a sleeveless long black with a slit on the right side. Luke smiles and went to put it on the bed, "hmm some privacy please."

"I can't leave you alone, but don't worry I'll look the other way." A low chuckle escapes.

"Why? Do you think I'm going to run away?" My voice, again, thick with sass.

"Yes, now go change." I'm shocked Luke would be so blunt. I walk into the bathroom and turn on the water for a shower. As the warm water pours over me, I feel refreshed. I never appreciate being able to shower until now. I finish cleaning up then slip on the dress.

"Luke!" No answer, "Luke!"

"Yes?" Luke appears in the doorway, "Woah. You're, beautiful." My face grows hot as Luke approaches me.

"Can you help me with the zipper?" I turn around. Luke steps closer, his fingers trace my spine down to my zipper.

I'm glad my back is turned, my face began to turn a shade of red. I feel his warm breath on my neck.

"All done." Luke's low voice brings a shiver to my body. Luke's hand lightly hovers around my waist as the other then traced the top of my shoulder. My back is pushed against his chest. I tilt my head as his lips lightly press against my neck.

"I thought we couldn't do this?" My breath heavy.

"I can stop if you want," he kisses my shoulder, "just tell me to stop."

I couldn't. I want to, but I couldn't. The feeling of Luke's lips against my skin makes all the strength I thought I had disappear. I try to focus on the fact of us dying if his boss finds out. But with Luke, it feels as if that doesn't matter, like nothing matters besides us. My family melts away, the mission is gone, the whole world dissolves with his touch. Luke turns me around and with an indescribable force, our lips clash. Luke presses me against the wall. I have nowhere to go, our kiss grew into a fight for air. Luke breaks free when he heard the door. "She's ready, bring the car around front."

"Yes, Sir." The man said.

"I'll meet you downstairs." Luke fixes his hair as he walks out of the room. My hand on my chest as I lean against the wall for support. This is going to end badly, I thought, as I walk out the door and to the car. Luke is leaning against the car his hair flows in the wind, he had a black suit with a black tie on. If this was my mission, why was he dressed up?

"Hey, why are you dressed up?"

"Change of plans, I'm accompanying you." Luke smiles, and opens the car door, "after you princess."

"Why? What changed?"

"My boss wants me to make sure you don't get hurt."

"Is there a high chance I could get hurt?"

"No, but just in case, I'll be your date tonight. So pretend that you like me." I roll my eyes, as the hotel disappears behind us. The man they want me to watch has importance to The Front. What is that? I need to talk to him, but with Luke, I wouldn't be able to. My mission is to talk to this man.

✳✳✳

It's nineteen hundred hours when John receives the phone call.

"John, I looked over your file." James said, "we'll help you."

"Thank you, can we meet tomorrow to go over the details?"

"No, I will be attending a charity in Belgium." James sighed, "you can meet the agent tomorrow. His name is Thomas Black."

"Okay thank you, I'll have my handler call tomorrow to set up a meet." He is good, John thought.

"Oh and John you need to start preparing. Finishing Project Maverick won't be easy, you need to read up."

"Yes, Sir." John sat on his bed and bowed his head. His eyes turn red as they filled with water. John hopes that Jacy remembers everything he taught her. How to fight, hide, and lie. She is his biggest priority. John starts to disassemble his gun and reassemble it. Focusing on each piece, how each part works together and that if one piece is missing the gun becomes a useless piece of metal. John knows he has to work with this Thomas kid. He knows that he needs him, even though he didn't like it. John wishes for a better option, where he wouldn't have to resume Project Maverick. John picks up the phone and dials.

"Hello?"

"Josh, this is John. I need you to do me a favor." John's eyes cold.

"Sure, what do you need?" Josh's voice confused.

"Go to the house and in my room, there's a button behind my dresser. When you press it, the side of the dresser will open to reveal a book. Grab it and hop on the plane, I need you here."

"Okay, I'm on my way."

"Gabriel is going to regret ever messing with my family," John said to himself.

Chapter 13

The Mission

The gold lights illuminate the ballroom floor. On one half of the room, there are tables and a buffet lining the side of the room. The room is crowded with men dressed in suits and women in elegant dresses. When Luke and I walk in we are approached by a couple, the man is young with blond hair, and the woman has long black hair.

"Luke, it's good to see you," the woman said, "who's this?"

"Hello, Jessica, and this is Jacy," Luke hesitates, "my girlfriend." I couldn't hide the shock I felt when those words escaped his lips. Jessica's eyes scanned me from head to toe, I could see jealousy arise in her eyes. She is pretty, her gold-toned skin and her perfectly framed face.

"Jacy, tell me about yourself," she said.

"Well, I'm 16. I have two brothers and," she raises her hand to stop me.

"Luke, can I talk to you?"

"Sure," Luke turns toward me, "I'll be right back."

Luke and Jessica went to the bar. I watch her closely to try and make out what she's saying. As I'm watching, a man walks in front of me.

"Hello," the man's deep voice carries in the room. This man is classically handsome, he looks to be around fifty years old, his black hair slicked back. This is the man in the picture, I wasn't supposed to get close to him. But here he is, offering me his arm.

"Hello," I reach out my hand, he did a half bow and lightly kisses my hand.

"I'm James Carter."

I'm about to tell him my name when Luke showed up. He stood between James and me.

"Hello James, I'm Daniel," I look back and forth between the two.

"I'm J..." Luke cuts me off.

"This is Jasmin," Luke gives me a scolding look, "how can I help you?"

"Jasmin, would you like to dance?" I know that it's a bad idea, but I wanted Luke to understand I could protect myself.

"Yes, Daniel hold my purse." I throw my purse at him as James escorts me to the floor. The more I thought about it... this is a good idea, I need to know why this man is important to Luke's boss.

"So, Jasmin what are you doing at this charity?" James twirls me around.

"I came with Daniel and his friends." I'm nervous, I could potentially be dancing with a murderer, "what are you doing here?"

"I came to donate," his eyes show recognition, he leans in, "This is a very seclusive party. Who is Daniel friends with to get into it?"

I look towards Luke. His eyes still fastened to me, while Jessica is doing the same. He must not trust me. "He's friends with a girl named Jessica."

James glances at Luke and Jessica, "oh I see."

I shouldn't have accepted the offer to dance, but its to late, now I'm stuck. I look back at Luke and see Jessica's hand touch his shoulder.

James twirls me around again. In an effort to get my attention. "You're not Jasmin. You're Jacy."

"No, I'm Jasmin," I back away, how does he know? I didn't say anything.

"No, you're not," I try to walk away, but his grip got tighter, "Jacy if you want to live, keep dancing."

"Okay, what do you want?" I want to run, I want Luke to step in but, he won't. I got myself into this mess and now I get out of it by myself.

"I want your boyfriend's boss, and John wants you." The sound of John's name makes my mind jump. John's here? Where? My eyes search the room before thinking, what if he's playing me?

"I don't know a John or Daniel's boss." I can't say, boyfriend, for the fact he isn't.

"John Carmichael?"

My eyes start to water, I blink them away. John is here to bring me back. I smile at the thought of home. "Who are you?"

"I'm the man who's going to bring you back to John." James said with a warm smile, "meet me tonight at the bar."

"Okay," James bows and walks away as Luke draws near. I'm safe I thought, Luke wraps his arm around my waist and guides me to the bar on the left side of the room.

"What did he say?" Luke's voice is filled with jealousy.

"He wanted to know how I felt about the charity," I feel bad for lying. If Luke knew what actually happened, he would keep me on lockdown. Luke grins and hands me a drink. I have to find a way to sneak out. Luke takes a swig of his drink, then takes my hand, "where are we going?"

"To dance," Luke pulls me close as a slow song began to play.

"Would you ever want to just escape from this life?" I smile, feeling the warmth of Luke's hand in mine. Guiding me around the floor.

Luke peers down into my eyes and smiles, "At this moment no, but check with me tomorrow?"

I laugh. "What time does this charity end?"

"I don't know. Are you tired?"

No, I'm excited. I have a chance to go home. "No, are you?"

Luke kisses my forehead. "No."

"Good." I blush even though I know its only part of his cover.

"You know, Jessica doesn't like you." He laughs.

"I figured. What's her problem anyway?" I attempt to hide my disgust, but Luke saw it, and he smiles.

"She says you're dangerous, and I should stay away from you."

"How?"

"I don't know, but," he caresses my face with one hand, "I don't think you're dangerous."

I smile and tilt my face into his hand. I couldn't leave Luke. I want him with me, I want him to be safe. I have to stay. I convinced myself.

✳✳✳

John make his way to the Westfield London Mall, where he is supposed to meet Thomas in the food court around noon. When John arrives, the mall is crowded which is good, this gives him a better escape option if he is followed or if it's a setup. John makes his way to the food court. He sits at a table that gives him a view of the floor. Within five minutes, a man approaches John.

"John? I'm Thomas Blake." Thomas's outstretched hand dangles in the air. John looks Thomas up and down before shaking it and gestures for Thomas to take a seat.

"Did James brief you?"

"Yes, but before I help. I have some ground rules." Thomas said.

"Okay, what are they?"

"This is my operation, you don't come out from behind the desk. Also, you need to trust me." Thomas's voice is subtle, yet stern.

John nods. "I also have rules. Rule one, don't get involved with her. Rule two, I am in control of the mission."

"Deal," Thomas scans the floors of the mall, "I'll be in touch to go over details tonight at headquarters." John nods his head, and just as John is about to leave, he turns to Thomas.

"Oh, and if you get Jacy hurt," John laughs as he slaps Thomas on the back, "I will kill you."

"Wouldn't expect anything less," Thomas smiles, "Do you have a picture of her?"

"Yes," John reaches into his pocket and pulls out a picture. Thomas's light brown eyes lighten, he ran his hand through his black hair. John quickly retracts the photo, "don't get any ideas."

"I wasn't," Thomas smiles, "I'll be in touch." Thomas watched John disappear in the crowd.

John fiddles with the thought of placing his sister's life in the hands of that boys, Thomas.

A few hours pass and John met with his handler. They discussed how to continue Project Maverick.

"So as soon as Jacy is safe, I'll go back undercover. You have to promise me you will make sure she gets home." John said.

"I promise."

"Josh will be arriving soon when he brings me my book, I can start preparing."

"Okay, when is your meeting with Thomas?"

"Any minute now," John stood up and checked his phone. "I'm heading there now, can you pick up Josh and bring him to my hotel?"

"Yes, and good luck."

"Thank you." John makes his way to SIS headquarters. As he made his way there, he thought of the first time Jacy and he went hiking. Jacy was twelve and John remembered when she got tired, he would give her a piggyback ride. Once they reached the top, they camped out. They looked at the stars, while John told stories about his adventures in Europe. John always had a plan to take her to Europe, but he never thought this was the way she would get to see Europe for the first time.

John heads to the same office. As he enters, Thomas stands up and greet John.

"Hello John, are you ready to go over details?"

"Yes."

"Okay, so I have intel that they will be arriving in London tomorrow."

"Do you know why they're here?"

"I'm guessing they know you're here. And that there is a dinner for one of their known associates."

"Is your source reliable?"

"Yes," Thomas gives John a reassuring nod, "don't worry I know what I'm doing."

"Okay, you're going to attend the dinner and how are you going to get Jacy?"

"I'll seduce her," Thomas smiles, knowing John wouldn't like the idea.

"No, find another way."

"It's the only way."

"No there has to be another way."

"Trust me... it's the only way. I promise I will be a gentleman," Thomas winks.

"If I hear you do anything, I will come in there myself and get her."

"I'll try to keep my hands to myself." John looks at his phone.

"Let me know when the dinner starts. I want to be there." John rapidly left the room. Josh has arrived in London.

Chapter 14

The Duo

It's dark, when I hear a gun in the distance. Men surround me. John's in the corner, a man stands behind him, I try to scream, but it's as if we are being separated by glass. The man raises a gun to John's head, tears stream down my face. I thrash trying to stop it, stop it.

I wake up covered in sweat, and tears in my eyes. My body is shaking, but whether it's from fear or adrenaline I don't know. It's only a dream, I have to keep repeating to myself. The dress I wore last night is on the hanger that hangs on the door. This brings me back to James Carter and last night. I could have escaped. I could have gone to John. After the dance, I tried to tell Luke, but his men were with us the rest of the night. I couldn't leave Luke, he has risked his life for mine to many times. I bite my lip at the thought of Luke, of our kiss. I mean kisses. He cares for me, he protects me. I need to return the favor, I need to help get him out of this organization. But how? I have to get Luke alone.

"Good morning, princess," Luke's smile is enchanting. I feel the rising heat in my cheeks as Luke came closer. But the heat quickly fades when his men follow closely behind him.

"I'm guessing it's time to go." I sit up slowly, my arms are placed behind me in support to keep me upright. Luke's eyes trail my face, which shows no interest in moving today. I'm exhausted from last night and all the training.

"Yes, it is, hurry up and get ready." Luke's voice is playful yet tense, "then we will get breakfast."

"How much time do I have?"

"Five minutes."

"Okay, now leave me to get ready." I toss my hand around dismissing them as if they are my servants. Luke lets out a low laugh that makes me smile.

"Oh, before I go, here are your clothes." Luke tosses them at me, I bat them away in a panic.

"You could have just handed them to me." I roll my eyes, but he had already left the room. I slowly slid out of bed, to put on my all-black outfit again. Luke has no style, including his men. I finish tying my combat boots, then I throw up a soft swept ponytail. I give myself a once-over in the mirror before I exit to go see Luke, whose room is next door to mine. I trudge over to his room, hoping that his men would be pulling the car around, or hauling bags down or something other than keeping an eye on me or Luke.

"Luke, you in there?" I knock once.

"Come on in." I enter the room to see Luke throwing on his black shirt. The light produces a shadow that enhances each muscle making them more defined if that were possible. I quickly turn around shading my flushed face, in hope that Luke didn't notice.

"See something you like?" Luke chuckles.

"No," I say, while slowly turning until my eyes met with his. I'm engulfed by the blue ocean in his eyes. I tore away from him in an effort to regain focus on what truly matters, escaping. Just as my mouth opens so does the door. This is just my luck, I smile in annoyance.

"The car is ready, Mr. Luke." A bulky man spoke.

"Thank you," Luke said, his voice is calm and polite, "Jacy, let's go."

"Okay, but since I got ready in the time limit. Could we get breakfast?" Luke's eyes bounce from me to his men, as though asking for permission. Isn't he in charge? My eyes start to trace his until a heavy sigh escapes his lips.

"Yes," Luke's smile is taunting, "hurry before I change my mind." I walk past him lightly running my shoulder into him. He smirks as his eyes follow me out the door. I look back to see Luke and his men trailing closely behind me.

James Carter, I need to find a way to get in contact with him, to see if he can help Luke, too. My mind races in circles realizing I didn't get his number or the organization he works for. Maybe he is lying. Maybe James Carter is the man that's after my brother, too? He said my brother John is here, and I know we are heading to London. Or are we?

It's 09:00 hours right now. If we stop and get food, it will be 14:00 by the time we arrive in London. My mind is rushed with thoughts, questions, and theories. But out of all those, there is one I need to know, is John really here?

Even though I've only been a *"spy"* for a week my observation skills have increased rapidly. When I walk into the restaurant, I see a layout of twenty circular tables, five chairs at each table. And along the walls are six square tables with two chairs at each, the kitchen on the right behind the cashier, which means a total of three exits. One in the kitchen, another by the bathrooms in the back and the front door. I scan the room in hopes of being placed between the bathrooms and the kitchen, this would give us a better escape route. Luke's smile shatters my focus, my eyes search his eyes, in the hope that I could get him alone. His eyes narrow, I seductively bite my lower lip. His eyes widen, then quickly return to normal as the hostess appears. I rotate my face away from him in embarrassment. Luke nudges me as she leads us to a table in the front of the restaurant. She hands Luke and me a menu. And when she attempts to give Luke's men a menu, they simply wave her off. Luke orders bread with honey and cheese, I order the same. It isn't long before it's presented to us. The bread is sweet and moist.

"We need to get going, the train leaves soon for London." Luke's voice is anxious.

"Okay, isn't there a later one?" Interest takes over my mind.

"No." Luke's voice intense.

"Okay, I'm ready to go." Luke places euros on the table then grabs my hand, and drags me out of the restaurant, and to the car.

"Let's drive." He orders his men. The car speeds forward at a rapid pace.

"Why are we in a rush?"

"Because we need to be in London at a certain time for my boss to be able to pick us up."

I shift my head slightly to the right, concerned. Luke places his hand on mine. As much as I hate to admit it, it's comforting. I intertwin my fingers with his, and that's when I see it. His face turning red, his breath quickens, his eyes beam like the sun as they peer at his feet, in embarrassment. I grin and lean in. He rapidly retracts his hand, my heart sunk at the feeling of absence in my hand. Luke's eyes meet mine, they are filled with pain.

I return the look with one thought running through my head, I need to help him.

✶✶✶

It's 22:00 when John rushes in the house that his handler has set up as a base. Josh is sitting at the table with a black book in his hand.

"Thank you for bringing that. Now you should go back home to keep track of Mama June," John attempts to snatch the book from Josh, "What are you doing?"

"John, I know I wasn't supposed to read." Josh stops abruptly as John interrupts.

"You read it!" John's voice is filled with anger, "You have to go home now."

"John, how are you still alive? Why didn't you tell me what you went through?"

"Because it's classified," John's eyes wander, "Yes, initiation into this, was painful, but I had to do it, and I have to go back."

"Why?"

"I made a deal, and a promise." John's eyes cold, "I need you safe to take care of Jacy when she gets back, so go home."

"No, I want to help."

"You can't. You could get killed." John's voice is laced with fear.

"So could you."

"That's different, now go home Mama June needs you right now."

"Actually, I brought her with me." Josh's smile is pleading.

"You what!" John yells.

Mama June appears around the corner. "I told him to, sweetie." Mama June said.

"You both will leave tomorrow."

"Okay, okay. We will leave tomorrow." Josh said. John walks over and gave Mama June a quick hug. He looks at his handler and motions for him to talk in private. John and his handler walk into a room and shut the door.

"Can you make sure they get to the airport on time? I have that dinner to oversee, with that Thomas kid."

"Yes and give the kid a chance. I hear great things about him." The handler said.

"Okay, I'll give him a chance. But no promises." John shrugs, "and thank you."

"Welcome, and good luck with your mission."

"Thank you," John smiles, and exit the room to see Josh and Mama June at the table. John makes his way over to them with one thought on his mind, *please stay safe.*

Chapter 15

Dead or Alive

It's 14:00 when we enter London. Luke has been distant ever since we were on the train when he got a phone call from his boss. I tried to talk to him, but he completely shut down. So we sat in silence. Every once in a while, I would scan Luke's face in an effort to read his mind. He would just look out the window with his blue eyes deep with sadness. And now in the town car, Luke still won't make any eye contact with me. With that, I couldn't help but wonder if his boss found out that, John is here? I search his face again, but this time instead of sadness it's fear. What is he scared of? Can Luke be scared? As long as I've known him, he has always been dauntless. From the time a kid twice his size attempted to take his lunch money, to the time his parents died in a car accident, and he had to be raised by his grandparents. Which he never talks about.

"So, Jacy we are going to go to a safe house called The Fort. Once there, you will get cleaned up. My boss wants us to attend dinner." His voice is cold. My eyes fill with anger, I haven't met his boss, and yet he's ordering me around, and he is taking the somewhat kind, and loving Luke away from me.

"No," I cross my arms, "I'm not doing anything for your boss."

"You have no choice," Luke's voice goes soft, his eyes draw down to his feet, "After this one, there will be no more, I will talk to him."

"No more after this one," at this point I'm not going to this dinner for his boss, but for Luke.

"Yes, no more." His eyes grow blissful when I slide my hand on to his.

"Fine, but I want something for doing this," as I speak his eyes turn curious.

"What do you want?"

"I want to call my brother," I smile. His face transforms into a mournful expression. Something's not right here.

"What's wrong?"

"Jacy, you know that phone call from earlier." Luke places his hand on my shoulder and scoots closer.

"Yes," my eyes narrow, as I tilt my head.

"Well I got some news," his voice creaks with pain, "It about your brother… he's dead."

The world disappears, my eyes swell. I see Luke's mouth moving, but all I heard was white noise. There's no way John could be dead, that man James Carter said that John was here in London. John can't be dead. Tears are rolling down my cheeks as I shake my head, "No!" I collapse into Luke. I grip his shirt, screaming into his chest. His strong arms wrap around me. His breathing synchronizes with mine. His heart is beating rapidly, I broke away. Luke's thumb gently wipes a tear off my cheek, as his hand cups my face, his blue eyes are drowning with sympathy, the corners of his mouth turn down.

"Everything will be okay." His voice was kind.

"Who did this?" I sniffed.

"A man named Thomas Blake. Thomas will be posing as an agent for the SIS or also known as MI6. Tonight this dinner we are going to." Something changes in his eyes when he speaks, his hand twitchs and his eyes dart away when he said Thomas is posing as an agent. Is he lying to me? Luke wouldn't lie to me, I thought in an effort to convince myself of it.

"What do you want me to do?"

"We just need you to keep an eye on him, but this time don't get close. Stay away, he's dangerous."

"Okay," my voice distant. I break away from Luke and peer out the window. Why would a guy from MI6 kill a CIA agent? This question runs through my mind as the tear stroll down my face. Something doesn't add up. John can't be gone.

When we pull into 'The Fort,' my head is pounding from the salty tears that poured down my face. I wipe them away when Luke's hand touches my shoulder.

"We're here." Luke speaks with a kind voice.

"Okay, thank you." I smile a courtesy smile, "when is the dinner?"

"Around," Luke looks at his black watch, "19:00, so we have an hour before we have to be there."

I nod my head in agreement. I step out of the car into a brisk breeze. The Fort is a one-story house, with bricks around the base complete with a sand-colored siding. I follow Luke through an oak door into a living room with the furniture cover with white sheets and the floor covered with dust.

"Which room am I staying in?"

"You will be in the room down the hall and to the left," Luke points, "I'll be just across the hall."

"Thank you," I try to smile, but it turns out to be dreary. My room has a single twin bed and a small dresser by the window. I turn to see Luke leaning in the doorway.

"Are you okay?" his eyes filled with compassion, his smile is amorous.

"I will be," I look into his eyes, "tell me how it happened."

"I don't think you should hear this." Luke shakes his head, as his eyes drop down to my feet then trace my body back up to my eyes.

"I need to know." I sit on the edge of the bed. Luke slowly makes his way over to me.

"I found out John was in London when we were on the road, that's why we were on our way here."

"Wait so you knew John was here before we arrived?"

"Yes, but after that, I got word that MI6 raided a CIA safe house," Luke said. John died because of me, if I had any fluid left in my body I probably would be crying. My head is throbbing from dehydration.

"Why would they raid a CIA safe house?"

"I don't know, my boss," Luke's look breaks my stare, "didn't give me the details."

"Did you see..." my voice choked, "the body?"

Luke's eyes drifted to the left. He shoved his fist in his pocket. "Yes."

Luke is lying, but about what? The way John died or that John is dead? I always watched a lot of detective shows when I was younger, and they always said no body no crime.

"I want to see the body," I say with a sense of urgency, and desperation.

"Let me make a call," Luke reaches into his pocket to pull out his phone but stops. He turns his head and gazes into my eyes, "I'll have my men bring you the dress for tonight."

"I don't think I can go."

"Yes, you can," his face deepens with frustration, "you have to, the man that killed your brother will be there. Don't you want to see him face to face?"

"No, what I want is to go back home," I spin until my back faced him. His footsteps are heavy as he walks up behind me. His powerful arms wrap around my waist, his head rests on my shoulder. His breath is warm. I feel a sense of ease in his arms, although I shouldn't. "Have you been lying to me?"

"It's not safe to talk here," He whispers into my ear, I shift my face over my shoulder. Luke tilts his until our eyes meet.

"John's alive?" I whisper. I reached my hand around to the side of his face. A shiver trickles down my spine, realizing how close he is, the heat from his body seeping into mine. Luke's face drew closer.

"Yes," A heavy sigh escapees his lips when they clash with mine. I spin around reaching my hands around his neck, drawing his face towards mine. His hand traces my spine down around my thighs and lifting me, my legs grasp around his waist as he presses me against the wall. A spark that grows into a flame every time our eyes meet.

"Sir? I have the dress." The door creaks open, Luke drops me, I grimace and give Luke a look that could have killed him, which he returned with a mouthed apology as he helps me back to my feet.

"Thank you, you can set it on the bed." It amazes me how Luke could turn from a man of mystery to a boy with a kind, caring, and loving heart. I lean against the wall and bite my lip, as I scanned the outline of his body. I rattle my head until I regained focus on what truly matters, John's not dead.

✳✳✳

It's 01:00 when John hears a blast outside of the base house, John reaches under his pillow and grasps a cold metal object. He slips his shoes on then quietly made his way into Josh and Mama June's room. He walks over to the cots, no one is there. John's heart drops, his grip grows tighter as he makes his way into his handler's room. John shakes the bed, his handler jumps. John lifts his finger to his lips. his handler nods his head, as he also pulls out a gun from his pillow. They slowly make their way out to the living area searching the house. Clearing every room until they come face to face with Josh and Mama June, tied down. There are three men, one by Josh the other by Mama June. The last man makes his way into the light.

"Gabriel," John raises the gun, tracking his every move.

"Hello to you, too," Gabriel smiles.

"What do you want?"

"I want revenge." He nods towards his men, they raise their guns.

"Revenge for what?" John's voice fueled with rage.

"Calm down. I won't hurt them," Gabriel lifts a hand, "I'm just using them to make a point."

"What is your point?"

"My point is they are family, I am family, so join me."

"Join you?" John forges a laugh, "no thanks."

"Join me in defeating your, I mean our uncle."

"Uncle Larry?" John's eyes fill with confusion.

"Yes," Gabriel starts a low laugh, "you don't know about him do you?"

"What about him?"

"He's what you CIA people call, Project Maverick."

"That impossible."

"Is it, though?" Gabriel's voice is taunting, "you've never caught him, and as soon as you think you're close he's always four steps ahead." John's eyes look from Josh to Mama June. Her eyes filled with tears, and his face pulled into a tight frown.

"If Uncle Larry is Project Maverick, then why did you take Jacy?"

"Oh I needed my sweet little cousin for a job," Gabriel's smile is condescending, "and since you trained her, I figured she would be a good asset, plus she's a good backup in case you don't join me."

"What do you mean back up if I don't join you?"

"She's trained by you. Therefore, she's just as good as you."

"What happens to my mom and brother if I don't join you?"

"Join me and you won't have to find out." Gabriel smiles.

John looks at his handler whose gun is fixed on the man by Josh. John's mind is employed by thoughts, *we could take them out, but there's no guarantee that they won't die.* "I'll take down Uncle Larry by myself thanks for the offer though," John said.

"I'll give you time to think about it." Gabriel snaps his fingers, his men instantly holster their guns while walking to Gabriel's side, "see you in two days."

John's eyes stern as he watches them leave. John sighs heavily, he places his gun in the back of his waistband, then ran to untie Mama June while his handler unties Josh. Mama June collapses into John's arms.

"I'm sorry mom," John said, his eyes filling with water.

"It's not your fault John," Mama June's voice is soft and comforting. John stands up and placed his hands on his head.

"I'm going to relocate you to a safe house," John looks at his handler, "don't tell me where you take them."

"What are you going to do?" Josh said.

"I'm going to get Jacy then" John takes a deep breath creating an absence of sound, "I will go after Gabriel and Uncle Larry."

Mama June and Josh began to pack, while John's handler gives him a contact within the SIS.

"Thomas will be your liaison for now."

"Okay, and thank you for everything," John walk them out the door and into the car, "I'll see you guys soon." As the car drives away, John reachs behind his back to feel his gun, and one thought enters his mind, *I am coming for you, Gabriel.*

Chapter 16

At First Sight

It's 20:00 hours when we arrive at the dinner. The building is like a historical landmark, beautiful. Gold lining around the hardwood floors, with a sunlight chandelier above the floor lighting the room. The stage with a band in the corner. Luke is wearing a black tie that enhances his grey suit, and his black shoes are polished with a shine that reflect the lights. Luke's suit is designed perfectly within his broad shoulders. I match his suit with a flowy light grey dress that stopped above my heels, the straps separated, exposing my back until the fabric reunites just above the small of my back. I search Luke's face admiring his strong jawline, his deep blue eyes, his golden skin, and his dirty blond hair perfectly fixed. Luke looks at me with a smile that brightens up my world.

"What are you looking at?" Luke said.

"Nothing important." I smile; Luke's eyes wander down my body as if he is memorizing every curve.

"So, tonight I'm not Luke, I'm Jackson, and you are Kacy." I nod.

"Okay, and are we a couple tonight or are we friends?"

"We will be friends. I have to do something tonight, so you will be on your own."

"So I'm like your back up?" I smile a taunting smile.

"Something like that," Luke shakes his head in irritation, "remember to stay away from Thomas."

"Okay," Luke pivots and starts to walk over to a woman near the table on the other side of the room. She is pretty, her long dark hair paired with a tall slim build. I roll my eyes when I see Luke rest his hand on her back as he guides her to a room in the back. I grab a glass of champagne when he disappears behind the door. Why did he have to go into a different room, with her. My face springs with jealousy. I take a gulp of the champagne; it's sweet like sugar and lemon. I find my table, it's two rows away from the ballroom floor. I sit there looking across the room I thought of earlier, how Luke lied. His boss wants me to think John is dead. Why? How would it benefit him if I thought John was dead? The only reasonable thought is to shift my reliance on Luke. The thought of Luke and that woman pops into my head as I take another gulp of champagne. I stare at the empty glass in disgust. Why would Luke need to get that close to that tall black-haired villain of a woman? I smirk at the thought that only villains have black hair.

"Excuse me, is this seat taken?" A low husky voice whispers in my ear, and sends a shiver that trickles down my spine, and my chest pounds as my eyes grew wide when I turn to see a man. His eyes are a piercing light brown that's framed by his rugged jawline, and his hair is short, layered dark chocolate that swoops into perfection. His smile with his golden skin seems, to light up the room. I open my mouth to speak but nothing comes out. My face turns a beet red. I slam my mouth shut and point at the seat next to me. He looks to be around seventeen or eighteen years old. He has a classic black suit on, that flawlessly frames his built body. I reach for more champagne as I admire his smile, but quickly I drink it all. Maybe it's the champagne that makes me think this man is an angel, perfect in every way. He let out a low laugh which breaks my focus. "Here let me get you another one."

"I. I'm…" I'm stuttering while clearing my throat. What is happening to me? "I'm good, thank you though."

He smiles as he nods his head. "How are you this evening," his smile is flirtatious.

"I'm good, How are you?" I fold my hands in my lap to keep them from shaking.

"I'm better now that I saw you," he smiles and snapps his fingers. A waiter appears with drinks. Smooth and powerful is the first assumption that rushes into my brain. He hands me a glass and he lightly sips his. I reciprocated his action as though to one-up him. "What's your name, beautiful?"

"It's... uhmm... Jacy," I stutter, "and yours?"

"Would you like to dance, Jacy?" My head shifts in confusion; he avoided my question. Who is he?

"No, thank you," I smile, "what's your name, handsome."

"If you dance with me, I'll tell you," he stands up. He's around six-foot-tall but with complete proportion. He reaches out his hand; I place mine in his and make our way to the floor.

"So, what's your name handsome?" I smile when he spins me into him.

"It's Thomas."

My eyes widen with terror as Luke returns to my mind. Thomas could be dangerous, and I told him my real name. I look into his eyes. *Stay calm*, I repeat to myself. Luke lied about John maybe he's also lying about Thomas. "Are you okay?" Thomas said.

"Oh, yes, I'm fine," I smile, "I think I had too much champagne." We dance in silence for the rest of the song. My mind is filled with questions, in hope that the man in front of me isn't a bad guy. When the song finishes, Thomas and I make our way back to the table. I felt guilty for being attracted to him. When we sit down, the first course is just about to be served.

"So, where are you from?" Thomas smiles.

"I'm from California," my eyes find his. They are ardent. I try to pull my eyes away from his, but I couldn't. They are stuck like glue.

"I know a guy from there," he slops towards me while setting his hand on mine.

"Who is it?" My voice is shaky, my face flushed with color. *Breath, just breath,* I repeat to myself.

"You wouldn't know him," Thomas's eyes break free from mine. His head tilts, "do you want to get out of here?" Without thinking, I nod my head, now on an adventure on my own just as Luke has left with that girl. Thomas grasps my hand and pulling me, I didn't know where he is taking me at first then I see the door. The same door Luke went through.

"I think someone is in there."

"No one's allowed in here besides the host," Thomas stops abruptly, I hit his solid chest, "and I'm the host." He opens the door and pulls me into a room that has a furnished red carpet with a bar in the corner and a card table in the center of the room. There are five men sitting around the table. The three men look around fifty, another look to be twenty-five with black hair and a beard. A dirty blond-haired man turns around, his eyes widen with anger. I thread my arm through Thomas's as Luke stares straight at him.

"Kacy?" Luke manipulates his voice, to sound confused.

"Hello gentlemen, deal me in." Thomas smiles as he laces his fingers with mine, and leads me to the table, "also Mr. Jackson, this is Jacy."

"Oh sorry, Sir." Luke's eyes burn a hole in me when Thomas and I sit beside him. My eyes attempt to escape Luke's. When Luke's glare meets mine, I read his mind; *what are you doing here?*

"It's all right, Jackson," Thomas must have sensed the tension because he then proceeds to place his arm around me. And whisper in my ear, "you look beautiful tonight." Without notice my face became warm, I smile nervously in an attempt to return my color back to normal. Luke rolls his ferocious eyes.

Tessa L. Gatz

"Let's play," Luke says with a smile that said two can play at this game. I shake my head lightly to try and tell Luke to back down. But he looks away. I didn't understand why Luke cared, after all, it's complicated. If he likes me, he dies. If I like him, he dies. If it's mutual, we die. I guess it wasn't that complicated, it was simple. There can't be a Luke and me.

It's around 23:00 when I intend to tell Thomas that I was ready to go, Luke didn't get my eye signals that I was ready to leave, and if he did then he must have ignored them. Luke had been looking from me to Thomas all night, especially when Thomas would whisper in my ear while holding my hand and wrapping his arm around me. For as long as I've known Luke, he's been a pro at hiding his emotion, but tonight with Thomas, it's as if all cards are on the table. Luke is jealous.

"Jacy are you ready to go?" Thomas said. He must have seen me close my eyes.

"Hmm?" I shake my head and force them open, "oh yes, only if you are."

"I'll drive you home," Thomas helps me out of my seat, I stumble into his chest.

"Wait," Luke said hastily, "one more round."

Thomas looks at me then shakes his head no. Luke's eyes fill with fire when he makes his way across the room, it might have been the champagne, but everything is moving in slow motion as Luke grabs my waist and pulling me into him. While getting a whiff of his sweet cologne. Thomas pulls me back with one hand while the other pushed Luke away.

"Hey, what's your deal." Thomas's voice is irritated.

"What's your problem," Luke repeats. Thomas didn't reply. He snaps his fingers and two men appear from nowhere.

"You two, stop," I push away from both of them and stomp towards the door, "I'm going to find my own way home."

"Jacy, wait." I hear Luke's voice ringing out from behind me. I fought the urge to turn around and make my way to Luke's men outside the club.

"Let's go," my voice demanding.

"What about Mr. Reynolds?" The driver said.

"He decided to play another game," I smile, "now can we go?"

"Yes, Miss Jacy." We pull away leaving Luke and Thomas at the front of the building. Luke's hands rest on his head, and Thomas's on his hips. I watch them began to argue before they disappear in the distance.

When I finally enter my hotel room, I collapse on my bed. My mind spins with questions. Why is Luke jealous? Why is Thomas so nice if he was supposed to be bad? And why can't I stay normal around either of them? The feeling of Luke's lips and Thomas's body made me smile. Why was Thomas so interested in me? Although it feels good for a night not to worry about John, Luke's boss or my family. I feel safer than I ever have before.

"Jacy, you awake?" Luke's voice is soft and quiet, as the door creaks open. I shut my eyes. I'm too tired to talk to him tonight. "If you are awake, I'm sorry. I... Don't know what happened to me tonight." I feel a blanket cover me, then the door slowly close as Luke whispers, "goodnight princess."

"Goodnight," I whisper once I'm surrounded by darkness. As I lay in bed, my mind crammed with thoughts of Thomas, and Luke. The thought of Thomas's eyes, his smile, his hand in mine, makes my stomach churn with guilt. When I remember Luke's eyes as they fill with disappointment and pain when Thomas wrap his arm around me. I knew Luke told me that Thomas is a bad guy, yet he also told me that John is dead. But, I couldn't help feeling as though I'm being pulled to him. I feel my eyelids grow heavy, and before I drift off into sleep I thought, *What am I going to do?*

Chapter 17

The Boss

The sun peeks through the white shades, and the sound of cars and people pour into the room. Along with a cool breeze. My eyes burn when the light hits them like a laser beam. I roll over to see Luke standing in the corner, my heart pounds.

"Sorry didn't mean to scare you." Luke slowly treated his way over to the bed, "How are you, princess?"

"I was good, then you called me princess," I smile, and I shift onto my side. Luke's eyes are bright even when he doesn't smile. They are refreshing.

"Well, hopefully, you get better because we have a big day for you," Luke gently pats my back while moaning in his struggle to stand up.

"Who's we?"

"You'll find out later today," Luke starts to open the door but then decides to turn around, "Also, before I go, can we talk?"

"Sure," my voice is distant, I already know what he wants to talk about, Thomas.

"So last night," Luke carefully paces his steps until he reaches the bed.

"Yes?" I try to hide the nervousness in my voice.

"Why were you with Thomas," Luke sits next to me on the bed.

"Well he approached me, and I didn't know it was Thomas until later, and by that time it was too late."

"Why did you give him your real name?"

I open my mouth trying to decide whether to tell him it's because I lost focus when I saw him, or because I was mad at him for leaving with that girl.

"First who was that girl you went with?"

"She helped me get into the back. I couldn't bring you along because I needed her to know I was available."

I roll my eyes. "Well, I told Thomas my real name because I was mad that you left me," the corners of my lips turn down, "Why did it matter if I was with Thomas. It's not like he would do anything in front of a crowd."

"Because he's dangerous."

"That's what you said when you lied about John's death. I don't know what to believe." Luke's face drew downwards with sadness.

"So, you don't trust me?" I freeze, I know I should say something, but I can't.

"I.." My voice cracks, and my eyes look towards the ceiling, "No, I don't."

Luke's eyes turn red. I move my hand over his. While searching his face in hope of trying to find something for me to say. But there's nothing.

"I better go." Luke stands up, and I suddenly feel an emptiness.

"Wait!" I scream dramatically, Luke raises an eyebrow, "Sorry, I don't know why I did that."

"Okay, see you in the car."

"No," I snap.

"What?" his voice fill with confusion. I slide out of bed still in the dress from last night and walk over to Luke with my chest puffed out as though I'm the powerful one.

"No," I cross my arms.

"Why not?" Luke takes a step closer.

"Because we can't leave."

"Why can't we?"

"Because we need to talk this out." I reach behind him and lock the door. Luke's face turns red as our bodies temporarily touched.

"Okay," Luke wraps his arm around my waist and pulling me closer, "Let's talk," Luke whispers into my ear.

I smile, debating whether to pull away or to continue his way of talking. Luke's face draws closer, my body is telling me to stay, but my mind is telling me to stop. I want to listen to my body, but I know I shouldn't. I turn away and take a step back. Luke looks at me confused.

"Before you do that, let's talk about…"

"Do what?" Luke stalks closer, his eyes hold a spark.

"You know what…" I smile while I back up slowly.

"I don't think I do."

"It doesn't matter…" I back into the wall, "I wanted us to talk, about how I do trust you, but I feel like you're always lying."

"Oh, princess, I would never lie to you" I have nowhere to go. Luke's hand slip behind my head, and just as our lips touch, there's a knock at the door. "I guess we'll have to continue this later."

"Sir, are you ready?" A man's voice said.

"Just a minute," Luke yells.

"I better go get changed." I duck past him and rush to the bathroom to change. I quickly throw on the same outfit they give me every day, and I put my hair up into a quick ponytail, then run out to meet Luke in the car.

We've been on the road for thirty minutes now. Luke hasn't told me where we are going, or when we would arrive. So, every now and then I would steal a glance at Luke while he directs the driver or stares at his phone. I attempt to look over at his phone, but he turns it away from me while a smile appears on his face.

"What are you doing?" Luke said.

"I'm bored, so who are you talking to?"

"My boss, he's going to meet us at the restaurant just up the block."

"I get to meet the guy that kidnapped me?" My voice heavy with sarcasm.

"Yes," Luke laughs, "We're here."

The cafe is small and local. There are two tables outside and a red lit sign that said open, flashing in the widow. When Luke and I walk in, the room is dim with lights slitting the difference between the floor and the ceiling. Round brown tables line the walls and in between them there are a pair of square tables that run down until the counter stops them. The counter is rustic yet new with one man behind it who seems to be inputting numbers. Luke directs me to a square table in middle of the room, to where a man sits. He's cleanly shaven with dark hair. Along with olive skin that seems greener in this lighting. Is this the boss? The man in the picture?

My cousin?

"Hello Jacy, Luke." He motions for us to take a seat, "I'm Gabriel."

"My cousin, right?" I said.

"Yes, Luke can you leave me and Jacy to talk."

"Yes, sir." Luke begins to stand up.

"Actually, can Luke stay?" I place my hand on his forearm as a hint for him to stay. Luke looks at Gabriel for permission. Which Gabriel allows. Luke quickly sits down. his eyes overflow with fear. I place my hand in his under the table, when our hands meet, he releases all the tension from his body. As did I, "So why am I here?"

"I brought you here because I have some bad news about your brother and your uncle." Gabriel possesses a calm powerful stance as he places his hands on the table.

"What about them?"

"John is dead. He decided not to help me, and I couldn't have him stop me from carrying out my agenda." I know John isn't dead, but he didn't know that, so I need to play along, my eyes start to water.

"You killed my brother?"

"No, I was wearing a nice suit that day. Your uncle did that."

"My uncle, killed my brother?" My voice is full of skepticism.

"Like I said he wanted to stop me instead of joining me." Gabriel smiled, "and I'm guessing he was doing the same to your uncle."

"Join you for what?"

"To get rid of Larry."

"Uncle Larry? Why?"

"Yes, and because he's trying to take over my business, and I can't have that, so I'm going to make you the same offer I made John and hope that I don't need my men to help you along with this decision." My eyes widen with terror as I hear the gun cock.

"This isn't part of the deal." Luke's voice is calm and shaky. I look over to see the gun targeted at his temple. I need to help him, but I also need more information.

"I'll join your team, but first I need to know who I'm working for." I put my hands up as though it would calm everyone down.

Gabriel looks at his man, and he retracts the gun from Luke's head. I interlace my fingers with his.

"You'll learn who you are working for in good time, but for now The Front welcomes you." Gabriel smiles and reaches into his pocket and pulls out a phone. "Here this is yours, I will be in touch with you about our next mission."

"Okay."

"Luke will be your superior, for now." Gabriel stands up and towers over Luke, "And, Luke, remember your place."

"Yes sir." Luke bows his head as Gabriel walks out of the room. I look at Luke, his eyes still filled with shock.

"Are you okay?" I said, with my hand in his.

"Yes," he drops my hand and rapidly stands up, "It's time to go."

"Okay," I feel incomplete without Luke's hand. I follow Luke to the car. I look out the window heading back to the Fort, the car ride is silent, and the air is heavy with fear and sadness. I take a look at Luke and only one thought has entered my mind, *I'm doing this for you.*

Chapter 18

The Fight

It's 02:00, when I hear a loud bang, my hearing splits into a constant whistle. I smell smoke; Luke enters my room yelling at me, but I hear nothing. Tears stream down my face. Luke grasps my hand and pulls me out of bed. I slip on my boots while Luke pulls out his gun, my hearing slowly starts to come back.

"Luke! What's happening?" I yell, Luke peeks over the top of the bed, his hands are shaking.

"They found us." Luke reaches behind me into a drawer that holds a gun. "Here take this."

"Who found us?" My eyes are struck wide, "why do I need this?" The cold metal brought a shiver down my spine.

"Because, we have to fight our way out." Luke's voice is low and quick, his eyes constantly search me, and the room. "You ready?"

"No! Who found us?"

Luke walks to the door, his forearms tense with the weight of the gun. I hold the gun at my side as I follow Luke out the door. I see a man down the hall, Luke raises his gun, he fires one shot, the man's body collapse to the ground. How can he do that? I sniff back the tears as we continue our way down the hall to the living area. I mimic Luke's every move.

"Luke, to the left." Without hesitation, the sound of the gun rings in my ears. My body began to shake, whether it's from adrenaline or from fear I didn't know. I look behind me to see a man approaching, I raise my gun, "Stop!" I shout. He grows closer, I close my eyes, as my finger wraps around the trigger, the gun jolts up as the bullet leaves the chamber. The man screams, I hit his arm. Before I could even think Luke fired a shot and the man goes silent as he falls to the ground. I look at Luke's his stern face, but his eyes shake with fear. I touch his shoulder; a low sigh escapes his lips.

"I'm sorry," his voice cracks. My hand falls off his shoulder while we continue into the living room. There are four men with automatic weapons and an older man in the back. They all have their weapons drawn. The older man walks forward to reveal his face, Uncle Larry.

"Jacy, sweetie." Uncle Larry opens his arms. Luke steps between Larry and me. His gun raised.

"Luke, it's okay. This is my Uncle," Luke shoots me a stern look, warning me.

"Luke, you better listen to her," Larry's voice is low sending a feeling of fright within me.

"She doesn't know what you do, she doesn't know any better." Luke places one hand behind his back grasping my shirt.

"What is he talking about?" I said. my voice is demanding.

"You don't know everything. All you know is what my stupid son told you," Uncle Larry sits on the couch, "here's the thing, I'm what you call undercover."

"What do you mean?"

"Well, long story short. I work for the CIA, I had to go deep undercover as a crime lord, internationally. And then I had an affair with a woman and then Gabriel actually became a crime lord." Uncle Larry's hand fly's around in exaggeration. I look at Luke knowing he isn't buying Larry's story.

"No, you actually are a crime lord, a gun runner, and drug king." Luke spits each word at him.

"Jacy, don't listen to Gabriel's little henchman." I narrow my eyes, Luke's in the same position I am in.

"If you're a good guy then why are your men still holding us at gunpoint," Luke smiles at me, it's comforting to see Luke smile.

"Because I don't trust Mr. Reynolds," Larry smirks.

Luke pulls my shirt forwards keeping me close.

"If he sets down his gun, then I'll tell my men to drop theirs." Larry smiles.

"No," Luke's voice echoes throughout the room, "Jacy and I are leaving, and if you try to follow us, I will shoot you." Luke pulls me behind him to the door while keeping his gun trained on Uncle Larry.

"Okay," Uncle Larry said, "But I'll see you soon, and Luke." Uncle Larry nods at one of his men and before I could open my mouth a bullet flies through the air. Luke screams, at the impact of the bullet. He falls into my arms; his jaw is clenched in pain.

"No!" tears stream down my face, my chest is heavy. My hand searches his body for blood. I see it trickle down his arm.

"It's al'right Jacy he just got my shoulder," Luke said, his body shivers in fear, as Larry walks over.

"That's a warning," Uncle Larry's voice is low and filled with anger, "next time just remember who you're talking to."

I place pressure on Luke's shoulder, once Uncle Larry disappears into a car, heading into the darkness.

"Jacy, everything will be okay, it's just a scratch." Luke wobbles to the ground. I lay his head over my lap, blood rolled down his fingers. Tears are running down my face, my hands shake as I try to apply pressure. Luke's eyes dim, "Jacy, call Gabriel." Luke said through cracked lips.

"Okay, but you have to stay awake." I frantically search for the phone. I pull it out, and just as I start to dial, a black herd of SUVs drive up. I look at Luke to see his eyes closed and his chest is still. I scream, "Help!" as I began to pump his chest. A man jumps out of the lead SUV. The light made a silhouette figure of the man.

"We need help over here." A deep voice rings with command. I couldn't count how many men and women jump out of their vehicles. A woman yanks me away from Luke, dragging me to the car. I thrash, knowing I couldn't leave his side.

"It's okay, Jacy, our team of doctors will take good care of him." The woman said.

"No! I can't leave him." My elbow flings through the air, as it connects with a hard bone. The woman's grip loosens just enough for me to break free. I Sprint towards Luke, four men try to grab me. I slide under the first one then return to my feet. The second one, my fist connects with his jaw, the man stumbles before falling to the ground as my foot hit his knee. The man screams in pain. I want to stop, but I know that if I stop, I would be caught. The air leaves my lungs, and a pain grows in my side and face as I hit the ground. I moan, the corners of my eyes turn blurry. A man walks beside me. My body told me to stop. I want to stop, but then the images of Luke rapidly shot through my mind like a movie. The first day we met, the day I arrived in Russia, and our first kiss. I can't quit, I spin on my side kicking in his knee. My head throbs with pain. I rush to my feet, breathing heavily. I pump my arms faster; Luke is only an arm's reach away when I hit what feels like a wall. My back hits the ground. I squint to see a man standing over me, Thomas.

Chapter 19

Need to Know

My eyes gaze at Thomas, analyzing him. What is he doing here? Why did he stop me? How do I get past him? I look around him to see a girl and three men preparing Luke to be hauled away, I narrow my eyes on his chest, hoping to see it rise and fall.

"Jacy," Thomas reach out a hand, "come with me." I need to help Luke, I sweep Thomas's legs out, then leap into a sprint.

"Luke!" I screech, then the truck starts to drive away. I pump my arms harder as though it could make me run faster. My chest tightens, and my legs start to give as the truck disappears in the distance. My knees collide with the cold ground. My chest feels like a weight, weighing down every breath. A darkness seeps into my chest. Luke is gone. I feel a hand linger on my shoulder.

"Jacy, come with me," Thomas said.

"Where's Luke?" My voice hoarse.

"Jacy, let's go." Thomas tries to lift me up, I jerk away.

"Where is Luke," I speak through gritted teeth.

"Luke is being transported to one of our naval medical bases twenty miles North of London." Thomas sighs heavily, while his hand runs through his hair, "now, Jacy. Let's go."

I slowly make my way to my feet; Thomas's men escort me to the back of a cargo truck. The men are all outfitted in a desert grey military outfit with a pistols holstered on their right hips, rifles sling across their chest. My eyes study them. They have either a gun or knife hidden under the base of their pants.

"Where's Thomas?" I ask. A man begins to close the back of the truck. He stops briefly, debating whether he should answer or not. "Where Is Thomas?" my voice is foreign, with a growling sound.

"He's…" The man's voice trailed off when one of the men in the truck shoots him a glance.

"He's where?" My eyes frantically search his body for direction, but the man didn't move, his face cold, his eyes dark. The light from the moon disappears as the man closes the back of the truck.

My body shivers. I didn't know if it's from the cold, or from the adrenaline as it dies down. I've been on the road for two hours and fifty-three minutes. Counting is the only way to keep me alert and my mind from thinking about Luke.

"Where are you taking me?" My head hangs looking over my red-coated hands. The blood from Luke has dried into a powder that stains my hands. I bring my eyes to meet one of Thomas's men. The man reaches towards his belt and pulls out a walkie-talkie.

"How far are we away from destination M?" There was static from the walkie.

"Four hours," a deep voice spoke.

"Is that Thomas?" I raise my voice, "Where is destination Marvel? Is that where Luke is?" I slam my foot on the bed of the truck. His eyes never waver from mine.

"No, that wasn't Thomas." His voice is short and deep.

"Where is destination M?" I know he wouldn't talk again, but I have to try. He leans back and adjusts his gun. Where is Thomas taking me? I brings my knees to my chest, a low moan escapes as a sharp pain in my knee sends a pain to my side and my head. *Three hours and two minutes.* The slits in the side of the truck allows a small beam of light to sneak through. I move into the little spots of light. The light glistened off my pale face, the man across from me spoke into his radio.

"Requesting permission to stop." The man's voice is low.

"Why?" The static make it sound like a woman's voice.

"The girl is cold," the man said.

"Permission granted," the woman's voice filters through the static. As the crisp air fills my lungs, I begin to wonder about Thomas. Who is he? And how did he know where we were? I thought back to the night I first met him. He is innocent, he is just a guy. And now I don't know who he is, or who he's involved with. The truck came to a halt, the guard stood up while motioning me towards the tail of the truck where another soldier opens the door to reveal Thomas and a woman. I know her, I didn't know how but I did. My eyes narrow as I try to place where I know her from.

"Jacy, honey, how are you?" Then it hits me, Jessica. I roll my eyes attempting to make her disappear. Thomas motions towards the guards. One of the guards position my hands behind my back, I try to yank them free of the guards, but a cold steel tightens on my wrists preventing me from breaking free. My breath quickens as the light disappears when a burlap bag was placed over my head. The men lift me out of the truck onto the ground where they guide me into a building. The air feels warm, and the floor is a tile, that sounds with each step of our boots. The men drag me down two corridors and into an elevator. I count the sound of each floor we pass. The elevator stops on floor twelve.

"Take her in here. And I'll go check with the doctors." Thomas's voice is low and demanding. I jerk backward as the men pull me into a room.

"Thomas!" I scream, "Thomas!" The metal door shut, locking me in. The men release my hands while returning my vision to see a small white room with a cot up against the wall. The lights illuminate the room to make an eerie feeling. My eyes dart toward the door to see Jessica standing, and observing. She holds a syringe that's filled with a blue liquid.

"Jacy, do you know what this is?" Jessica stalks closer.

"Where's Thomas? And Luke?" My eyes are glued to the syringe.

"It's a drug that is still in its experimental phase, and only available on the black market." Jessica flicks the syringe, releasing a drop of the liquid on the floor.

"What does it do?" The back of my knees hit the edge of the cot. I couldn't move.

"I don't know, yet." She nods at the guard; their hands wrap around my arms holding me in place. The needle pierced my neck, my eyes blur with tears and my fingers began to tingle at the tips. The guards place me on the cot, the light begins to flicker. I attempt to regain focus, but it is no use my head hit the pillow, as I watch Jessica walk out the door, and out just before the door closes, I see a man.

"John?" I whisper as the light fades and the heavy metal door closes with a sound that echoes throughout the room. Only one thought enters my mind, *I'm safe.*

✷✷✷

The pain is unbearable, I scream as the doctor's work on my wound. My head becomes light as the blood drips down my arm. The bullet is lodged in my scapula. My eyes search my surroundings, I'm in what looks like a mobile medical facility. There are four doctors, one holding my head, the other is strapping my legs and chest in, while the other two stands on either side of me, with scalpels and a tube that suck blood into what looked like a plastic bag. I could feel my body starting to faint from blood loss. My eyes close to reveal a picture of a girl. She is majestic, like a princess from a movie. Her hair is a light brown that stops in the middle of her back, her eyes a green with a hint of sun stirs into the iris. Her skin is a light bronze. Jacy, I try to call for her, but no sound came out. She turns her head to a man, he has a gun.

"JACY!" My body thrash against the restraints, I gasp for air. My eyes widen in pain, the doctor behind me places a sock in my mouth.

"Why do we have to save this kid, he's working for the enemy." A man with bright blue eyes said in an irritating voice.

"Because this kid, can help us, and Commander Blake said he wanted to talk to him himself." The brown-eyed doctor says with anticipation.

"What for? He has that girl that he can use." My chest aches at the thought of Thomas having Jacy. *I need to help her.* I try to get up, but my vision is blurry. My body relaxes, to see Jacy strapped down, tears rolling down her face. A man approaches her, slowly. His hand wraps around a silver metal gun. She's screaming, as he lifts his hand, and brings it down across her face. Blood drips from her lips, her eyes trace over to mine. The sun that was once there is fading.

My vision returns, to see a blinding light. I throw my head back and arch my back as the doctor takes a pair of forceps and dig into my shoulder.

"Almost got it," The doctor with brown eyes speaks with a strained voice. My body relaxes as I release a breath of relief. My eyes water when I see the bullet in his forceps. The relief of pain is brief. The doctor hands the other doctor a suture kit. My body tingles as my eyes closes to display Jacy standing in a room. The walls are grey, and the tile is white. There are two rows of beds. Her hair pulls into a perfect ponytail, her eyes are red from tears, a man walks over to her. The man opens his arms embracing her. My heart drops, as his hand caresses her jaw, lifting her chin until her eyes meet his.

"He's gone." Jacy's voice creaks, the man nods. I try to yell, *I'm here. I'm alive.* No sound. I try to move, but I can't.

"I know, but I am." The man's voice is soft and gentle, as he leans in, placing a soft kiss on her lips. Then pulling her into his chest. My chest aches at the sight of her with someone else. The picture slowly fade into darkness, as I thought, *Jacy don't give up on me. I'm Alive.*

Chapter 20

The Prison

My head is pounding with a thousand hammers and my body is bruised. Trying to sit up is like lifting a box of rocks, hard and painful. I open my eyes to a blurry figure standing in the corner. I blink trying to clear my vision. The figure is tall and thin. Its hair is either a black or a brown, and it is long. Jessica.

"What did you give me?" I swing my legs over the edge, every moment is straining.

"Something to help you relax and sleep." Her voice is oppressive.

"Where's Luke?" I pinch the brim of my nose as though it would make a headache disappear. Jessica walks over and gives me a cup filled with two pills. "What is this?"

"It's medication to help with the pain," she points at my head and side. I bow my head and smile while pushing the medication away.

"I was always taught don't take meds from strangers," I smirk.

Jessica places her hand on the grip of the gun that stays holstered at her hip. She wears a sand yellow tank-top with a pair of black cargo pants. Her piercing green eyes study mine. Her lips slowly turn into a grin.

"Thomas will be here in a minute," she said. Then promptly turns around throwing her hair into a perfect circle. She turns to face me one last time before leaving the room, "Oh, and Luke is safe."

My heart pounds at the sound of Luke being safe. "Before you go, can I ask you a question?" I say still with the thought of Luke on my mind.

"Yes," Jessica crossed her arms, as though she is ready to defend herself.

"You were at that dinner when Luke said... You know... We were together right?" Jessica nods her head. "How do you know Luke?"

"I met him when I was younger. We grew up together." Jessica's eyes drift towards the floor, "after his parents died in that car accident as you know he went to live with his grandparents. And they weren't the normal loving grandparents. They were hard on him, so he became secretive and distant. And when I was 8, I saw him at an arcade. I asked him if he wanted to play, and, well, long story short we became friends and grew up together. Then one night a man approached Luke and me with an offer, he didn't tell me his name but he knew everything about me and Luke. He offered me a new life, and Luke the same. I wanted Luke to have a new life, so I agreed and so did he. And that's how we met." She sighed and nodded her head.

"That man was Gabriel right?" I prod.

"He never told us his name. He just offered us a new life, together." Her eyes lighten at the word 'together' were they together? My stomach flips at the thought. Even though I know he has been with others, but just the idea of his lips touching hers makes my chest ache.

"Were you guys... Together?" I mumble.

"No," I relax letting my breath slowly seep out from between my lips, Jessica let out a low laugh noticing that I'm relieved. I bow my head in embarrassment.

"Can you tell me where Luke is?" I look up, to see Jessica opening the door to reveal Thomas standing the door way. His chest puffed out and his eyes are challenging.

"No, she can't." Thomas's voice is stern as are his eyes. He motions at Jessica to leave. She nods respectfully and without hesitation left the room. I look at Thomas, my heart jumps to my ears. He leans against the wall. I shift my body uncomfortably. Thomas's eyes lock with mine. The silence in the room brings a tension of unspoken emotions. "Jacy."

"Yes?" I tear my eyes away, when he starts to stalk towards me. I moan in my panic to stand up. Pain shot across my face.

"Are you okay?" His hands reach out to stabilize me, but I move away. His eyes fill with hurt as he retracts his hand back across his broad chest.

"Yes," I force a smile. I thought it would help break the tension but instead, it grows.

"Jacy, are you scared of me?" His eyes scan my face and my body. "Do you think I'm a bad guy?"

"No, I'm not scared of you." I didn't lie, I'm not scared, I didn't trust him. I don't know who he is, or how he knows where Luke and I were. And he's been keeping me in the dark. I bring my lips into a stern line, knowing that if he know that I didn't trust him he might slip up and give me an answer to at least one of my question, like where is Luke? Or Who are you? And who do you work for? "Are you a bad guy?"

"No, I work for the SIS, also known as MI6." He walks closer, this time I didn't move. Even though I want to, I couldn't. Maybe it's his eyes that draw me in.

"How do I know you're not lying?" I walk so that my body is parallel to the cot while keeping eye contact with him. His lip curl upwards revealing a smile, my chest pounds. I scold myself for being weak and falling into the hero persona that he displays perfectly.

"Because I have someone here who asked me for help in getting you back." Thomas looks back at the door, as it opens a man walks in, my eyes start to swell without thinking I run over to him, wrapping my arms around him.

"John, I'm so happy to see you." My voice choke, and tears rolling into his shoulder.

"I'm happy to see you, too, kiddo." His voice is comforting. I feel safe in his arms, but a small feeling arrives in my gut telling me it wouldn't last for long. John pulls away.

"What are you doing here?"

"I came to make sure you were safe," John's eyes dart away from mine, "Jacy, I made a deal with Thomas's agency, I have to leave. Don't ask any questions because I can't tell you where I'm going or what I will be doing. But you do need to know this, Thomas is here to keep you safe until I get back."

"When do you leave?" My head spun with questions.

"Now," He mumbles, "I'll be back as soon as I can until then I'm trusting Thomas to keep you safe. That means keeping you away from that Luke kid, Okay."

"No, not okay. Luke is in the same position I'm in, captured by the enemy. Where is he?." I broke free from John, running my fingers through my hair. I need to help Luke; we need to help him.

"Jacy, whatever Luke told you was a lie. He joined Gabriel. He's Gabriels second in command." I shake my head, no he can't be. Gabriel points a gun to his head.

"It's not true, Gabriel pointed a gun to his head." My mouth drops at the realization of what I did. I turn slowly to face Thomas and John, "I said yes, to Gabriel. To save Luke. I'm a part of the front."

"You're what?" John throws his hands in the air then turns to Thomas, "you need to lock down this place, Gabriel probably already knows they're here." My eyes widen at the word they. Luke's here?

"Wait what do you mean by 'they are here'?"

John ignores my comment, focusing on Thomas.

"Don't worry, I have it under control," Thomas reassures him as a guard walks in.

"Time to go," The guard spoke. John nods and starts toward the door.

"Jacy, I'm sorry I put you through this." Just as I'm about to talk he was gone. All that was left was Thomas. I went to sit on the cot, my head spins trying to comprehend what just happened. Thomas's hand touches mine, stopping me. My body wants to know what he was going to do, but I know it's just because I'm upset. I fight the urge to stay and keep walking.

"I'll come back and get you for lunch," Thomas said just before the metal door closes. Leaving me alone with my thoughts.

***

I wake up to pounding water being poured over me. I open my eyes while gasping for air. The water stops to reveal a man I'd never seen before. He is tall and lean, with greenish-hazel eyes. There are indents in the bridge of his nose, suggesting that he wear glasses.

"Let's start with an easy question," The man said as he drags a chair over, making a sound of metal scraping against the cement floor. My eyes search the room noticing every detail. The room has a staircase to the right, told me the room is underground, along with the cobwebs in the corner and the damage cement walls. Also, the temperature is cold enough that the water that soaks my body was steaming. I shiver and smile.

"My name?" I chuckle, "It's Daniel Long. what's your name?"

The man smiles pulling a gun out from behind his back. The gun has a military grade grip, this man is a professional, and serve in the military.

"Luke, lying is not a good start to our friendship." He shakes his head.

"I'm sorry, pal, but what's your name again?" I tilt my head.

"I didn't say, but you Luke are something else," he snaps and a woman I know too well appearing with a file, Jessica. Jessica hands the man the file. "According to your file your parents died when you were younger leaving you with your grandparents. Which then led you to join an organization called 'The Front'."

"Seems like you already know everything, so why am I here?" I narrow my eyes, trying to read him and see if Jessica is sending me a message. She taps her arm then the next time she holds it out, Morse code. Dot, line, line, line means J.

Dot, line, A. Line, dot, Line, dot, C. Line, dot, line, line, Y. Jacy, they have Jacy.

"You are here because of your connection to your boss." He shuts the folder.

"Oh, it's not because of a girl?" I smile instantly seeing the anger boil up in his eyes. His face starts to turn red. He walks over to me and places his hand on my shoulder. I bite my lip to keep from screaming.

"Now, why did you have to do that… I thought we were friends." The man releases my shoulder, snapping his fingers for a towel to wipe away the blood. Jessica rushes over handing him a cloth, then whispering into his ear. His face fills with joy. He glances back at me, "Sorry to cut this visit short, but I have other matters to attend to."

The man promptly walks over to a table in the corner, he reaches down to grab a syringe, filled with a light blue liquid and handing it over to Jessica. She slowly walks over to me, and pierce my neck, injecting me with the liquid.

"What is that?" I rotate my neck trying to work out the pain. She ignores me and follows the man out of the room leaving me with the sound of clinking pipes. My body shakes, and my eyes become heavy. I try to stay alert by thinking of what Gabriel could be planning or why Jessica would be here. She never goes into the field; she always stays with Gabriel. My mind starts to drift to Jacy, Jessica knows where she is, and that man has some sort of relation to her by the way he reacted. He's not an old boyfriend because his eyes didn't fill excitement, or hurt at the thought of her, so must be a brother or father. My fingers start to tingle as my eyes shut revealing nothing but darkness, and a single thought, *I need to talk to Jessica.*

Chapter 21

Project Maverick

I sit on my bed looking at the white walls, dreaming of home. When it was simple, wake up, go to school, come home to Mama June, Josh, and Grandma Gin. Then hang with Kim, Madison, and Luke. I hope he's okay. I think back to the night when Thomas's men took him away, and then to today, when John said 'they'. Thomas knows where he is, but he won't tell me, but if Jessica is still with Gabriel maybe I can get her to at least tell me if he's still alive.

"Jacy, are you ready?" Thomas peeks half of his body through the door. His light chocolate eyes search my body. I slowly stand up trying not to show pain, but the pain is overwhelming, I start to wobble. Thomas rushes over and grabs my arm and places his arm around my waist, instantly steadying me. I squirm out of his grip.

"What are you doing?" He holds his hand out as a look of confusion appears on his face.

"I was trying to help you," his voice is filled with annoyance.

"Well stop, I don't need your help." I lean against the wall.

"It looks like you do," Thomas smirks, and shrugs his shoulders while walking towards me. My face grows hot with anger, at the thought of him thinking that I'm weak.

"I'm not weak, I don't need help." My voice is irritated.

"Oh you're right, you're not weak... you're strong and stubborn, which means you don't know when to stop and ask for help." Thomas places his palm on the wall. His face close to mine, his eyes constantly searching and his mind calculating. Thomas is around six foot. His bicep stands out, as he leans in closer, placing all his weight on one arm. His other hand slowly moves to my arm, gently skimming the skin until it reaches my face.

"I'm… I'm not stubborn," My anger vanishes as he moves my hair behind my ear. I feel small in the little space we have.

"Okay, whatever you say," He smiles and leans in closer letting the air from his lungs fill mine. We stay there for a minute then he smiles and pulls away, "Ready?"

"Hmm," I couldn't think of the words. I nod while scolding myself for falling into the trap. Thomas guides me out the door into a corridor. It's filled with doors with two guards stationed by each one. He leads me down two halls and into a room filled with lines of tables, and a long line of people moving slowly towards an opening in the wall, and above the opening, there's a chalkboard that said 'hamburgers, fries, tots, pizza, and potatoes.'

"What would you like to eat?" Thomas asks as we walk past the long line to the front.

"Just some fries," I smile, the pain spread throughout my body. I rock onto Thomas, then quickly stand straight up. He must have notice; he begins to search the room for an open seat.

"Over here," he guides me to a seat at the front of the room, "stay here, I'll go get your food."

"Okay, I'll try not to limp away to freedom." I roll my eyes; he smiles then rushes to get the food. I'm sitting by two boys and a girl. Both of the boys have auburn hair, but one has a scar above the right eye. And the girl has short black hair, with dark green eyes. They whisper back and forth with each other. The girl looks me up and down before continuing to whisper.

"She's the one…. I heard Commander Blake is… and she was with…" The girl said.

I try to eavesdrop, but she keeps getting quieter.

"Excuse me, can I help you?" I roll my eyes. The boys look from her to me.

"Actually, yes, I have some questions for you."

I nod my head.

"How did you escape captivity?"

"I didn't. Thomas found us." I keep eye contact with her.

"So it's true you were involved with the enemy."

"No, I'm not involved with the enemy." I narrow my eyes, knowing she thought Luke was the bad guy.

"Hmm okay so is it true you joined the enemy for some guy you fell in love with? Also is it true that you and Commander Blake got together while you were engaged with the enemy?" She smiles, as shock covers my face.

"No, and no." I could tell she didn't believe me. She turned toward the boys trying to get them to ask the questions, but fear arose in their eyes.

"Okay, so I have one last question," she looked past me to Thomas, "How did you get commander Blake to bend over for you." She motions to Thomas who has a plate in his hands.

"I didn't do anything. He was given orders." I shrug and look back at the girl, she smiles and motions towards the door. The boys stand up and follow her out just as Thomas places a tray of fries in front of me.

"Were they bothering you?" Thomas's eyes trace them out the door.

"No, they had some questions, and well, I have nothing to hide," Thomas's smile is comforting. He reaches over and grabs a fry.

"Do you trust me?" He whispers. I look into his eyes, and I got a strange feeling that almost feels misplaced.

I nod slowly, Thomas searches the room fanatically while grabbing my hand pulling me, I groan in pain while biting my cheek to keep me from screaming. He pulls me down two hallways filled with guards. By the time we enter an empty room, I could taste blood. Thomas stops, his eyes frantically search the room. I look around wondering what he's looking for. "I need you to trust me."

"Okay," I lift an eyebrow. He looks around one more time.

"I think your brother is in danger, and I think there's a mole in the system." He looks genuinely concerned. I nod my head knowing who he is talking about, Jessica. "But the only way to know for sure is to talk to Luke, and I know he won't talk to me."

"You want me to talk to Luke?" I try to hide my excitement. Yet I have a strange feeling this would be more for Thomas then for me. "Why?"

"Yes, you are the only one he will talk too."

I lower my eyes knowing that I'm not the only one. Luke would talk to Jessica, but I'm not going to tell him that. I need to know where he is. I need to help him, and if Thomas knows Jessica could do the same thing I could do, I wouldn't get the chance to see him.

I nod. He runs his hand through his hair, fixing it, as well as fixing his uniform. He smiles and takes my hand as he walks me back to my room. Once I enter my room, I collapse on my cot. Thomas leaves as soon as my body hit the cot. I stare at the ceiling thinking of Luke, and Jessica. I closed my eyes, letting my body relax as I fell into a deep sleep.

✱✱✱

My eyes opened to Jessica tapping the side of my face. I shook my head trying to remember what had happened.

"Luke, they have Jacy on the twelfth floor. Gabriel is planning a raid on the base in four days at zero two hundred." I blinked trying to regain my focus. The drug they gave me must still be in my system.

"Is she okay?" My voice is hoarse. My body shivers and I began to cough. Jessica gives me a pill and a glass of water. "What is this?"

"It's a thermal pill, military divers use it to keep their core temp at a certain level so that they don't become hypothermic." I nod my head then gulped down the pill.

"Jessica you need to help me get out so that I can get Jacy out." She nods and leans in to slip a knife in my hands behind my back. I mouth thank you.

"I have to go talk to Jacy, and Luke, be careful okay." I nod as she disappears. I take the knife and start to saw at the rope that secures my hands behind my back. I look around the room trying to remember what day it is, or what time it is.

"Hello Luke," The man enters the room with a file in his hand, as he draws closer I see the file name, 'Project Maverick'.

"Hey, so how is that girl doing? She's probably missing me right?" I smirk.

"She's doing good and now knowing who you really are."

"And who might that be?"

"The enemy."

"The enemy really?" I let out a low laugh.

"Yes, and now that she knows. She has to move on to a better guy." He smiles.

"Sure she did, or maybe she's making you think she has?" My smile fades when the man pulls out a picture that shows the back of a man, pining Jacy against a wall, there's no space between them. I look away, as my heart drops. The man places the picture on the chair, then leaves, my head spins with denial. I kick the chair away. They tricked her, she doesn't know any better. I scream in anger. I have to talk to her. There must be a reasonable explanation. My eyes fill tears. There must be an explanation. I sigh and look towards the door, there must be.

Chapter 22

The Light

I don't know what time it is when I wake up. There are no windows in my room, which I think now of like a cell. I pace back and forth, thinking of what I would say to Luke if I will get to see him. I look at the door as Jessica comes barging in. Her eyes scan the room.

"Jessica, what's wrong?" She places her finger on her lips. She walks over to the corner above the cot. She leaps on the cot; her hand reaches towards her hip where she pulled out a knife. She dug into the wall and pulled out a long cord with a camera on the end. She took the knife and cut it across the cord severing the wires.

"Jacy, Gabriel is coming to get us in two days." her voice is low.

"What do you mean by us? Aren't you supposed to be on Thomas's side?" I cross my arms.

"No, Gabriel placed me here, he thought you and Luke would get caught at some point. And turns out he was right. So that's why he's coming to get you and Luke." She jumps off the bed, walking over to me. "Listen closely, Gabriel needs you and Luke to be able to take down Larry. Also, he thinks that my cover is blown, so I'm leaving tomorrow."

"Wait, what?" Everything is spinning around. Mostly with information that I don't even know whether it is true or not.

"I know this is a lot, but you need to focus. Luke is being held in the basement, and when Thomas takes you down there. Luke is going to take you hostage, okay."

I nod. "Wait, why can't you just tell Thomas about Gabriel and Larry. Thomas might be able to help?"

She shook her head. "Thomas can't know. Gabriel is off the grid, and if Thomas finds out about who really is behind Project Maverick, he will lose all faith in his government and in his co-workers. And Gabriel can't have that. He needs him to keep digging, to uncover the truth."

I take a step back. "What is Project Maverick?"

"It's a mission that was given to Gabriel to take down Larry."

Gabriel is an agent? I nod and look at her. "So Gabriel is an agent with the SIS?"

She nods, then looks at the door. "I have to go," she walks past me bumping my shoulder, "remember Thomas can't know," and with that she left. Leaving me alone with a tiny hole in my wall, and a headache. I sit on the cot, massaging my temples trying to remember everything, and comprehend it. Luke is in the basement, which is approximately thirteen floors down. I close my eyes trying to remember the floor plan. Then I remember, Thomas might bring me down there either today or tomorrow, but the raid is in two days. Jessica left, this is now on me, and Gabriel is counting on it. If he really is a good guy, then I'm doing the right thing. If he's not, then I'm ruining everything Thomas and John have worked for. Which is what? My stomach turns at the thought of getting it wrong. Luke's life and my life depends on this decision.

I pace for hours, thinking of Luke, Thomas, John, Larry, and Gabriel. How can they all claim to be good? I thought from when I first found out about John being an agent within the CIA to my first time in Russia with Luke, to my first meeting with Thomas then Gabriel, and when Larry shot Luke. I couldn't trust anyone anymore, not even my own brother.

"Jacy, are you ready?" Thomas enters the room, my eyes widen. He carries a flashy smile, showing off his perfectly aligned teeth.

"Sure," I smile trying to show off mine.

"What's wrong?" Thomas tilts his head letting the sparkle of white disappear and turn into a concerned frown.

"Nothing," I shake my head thinking that since I'm talking to Luke for him, maybe he will tell me about Project Maverick, but then I remember about what Jessica said.

"Something's wrong," Thomas shut the door and slides his hands into his pockets.

"I saw a file called Project Maverick. Can you tell me what it is?" Thomas's face shows no emotion, not even recognition of the file name. He marches over to me grabbing my hand and searching my face with his eyes.

"It's the project your brother is working on. And that is all I can say," he gently threaded my hand through his arm then escorts me to the same dining hall as yesterday.

There are more people in the hall today. I look across the room, looking for an open seat, or table. Thomas points at a table along the far side of the room. There are two open seats. I nod, not knowing if they will still be there after we got our food. Thomas navigates me through all the sea of people.

"Thomas? Shouldn't we wait in line?" I point at the line.

"Do you guys mind if we cut?" Thomas smiles at the men and woman behind us.

"No, Sir," they said in unison. Thomas smiles at me then gives them a nod. Once we hit the front of the line, the cooks have the meal fully prepared. It's a sandwich filled with cheesy eggs with bits of bacon and sausage in it.

"Hmm, you got a lot of pull here." I look around now noticing that everyone is watching us. "Thomas, everyone is watching us." Thomas looks around.

"Actually, they're watching you." Thomas winks, my face grew warm.

"Why?" I lower my head and drop slide my arm out of Thomas's, hoping this could make me less visible.

Thomas shrugs and places the tray on the table. "So, you will meet with Luke tomorrow night."

"Okay," butterflies fill my stomach at the thought of Luke. I took a bite of the sandwich, I shut my eyes savoring the taste. Thomas laughs at the pleasure I take from the warmth of the sandwich. His smile is kind. I look around the room in hope that no one is still staring. Sure enough, they are. I bow my head in embarrassment.

"Want to go someplace else?" Thomas must have seen how uncomfortable I am. I nod slowly. Thomas grabs my hand, and I grab the tray. He leads me back to my room. I look up the corner, where Jessica had ripped a camera out of the wall. The hole is now patched, I wonder if Thomas notices the bright new white that hangs in the corner and if he did, why isn't he mentioning it. He must know Jessica is gone by now, but if he did, he wouldn't need me to talk to Luke. How could she leave without anyone knowing? My heart jumps when I feel Thomas's hand pull me further into the room. He takes the tray and places it on a side table that I've never seen before.

"When did you get this?" I point at the table.

"Earlier this morning, they wanted it to feel homey for you." He places finger quotations around the word 'homey.' I look around the room, no matter what they put in here it won't ever feel like my home, it just feels more like a cell with a few luxuries. I laugh at the thought of my definition of luxury. My eyes begin to burn as I feel a tear start to appear. I didn't know why I'm crying. Thomas lifts his hand to my cheek, and with his thumb gently wipes away the tear. His hands are callused yet soft, his eyes shine as well as his smile. As they fall to my lips. I bite my lip slightly while tilting my head into the palm of his hand. One hand pulling my waist bringing my body into his, while the other hand slips behind my neck drawing my face into his. His lips are soft. His kiss is tender as though it could break at any moment. I lift my arms around his neck. My body tingles with an indescribable feeling of *it's meant to be.* Thomas pulls his face away just enough so that I could see the lust forming in his eyes. His smile is filled with ease. For some reason, this felt right, which is different from Luke. With Luke, it's exciting and dangerous. I never know what he is thinking, but with Thomas, it's easy and simple.

"I think my sandwich is cold." I laugh into his chest.

"Oh well," Thomas winks while dropping his hands from my body. "I better get back to work, but don't forget about tomorrow." Then Thomas disappears. I collapse on the cot staring at the ceiling, thinking. What am I going to do?

✳✳✳

My eyes water as I finish cutting the restraints. I look at that picture trying not to make too much noise, I place my arm across my body, placing my thumb in my belt loop as a make shift sling to keep my arm stable. The pain spreads throughout my body. I bite my lip drawing blood. I look at my wound, which was oozing a greyish green liquid. I sigh, knowing that it's infected. I walk over to the door where Jessica had exited, I figure there would be guards outside. I look around the room trying to find an air duct or a window to escape from but, I'm completely isolated.

"Is he asleep?" A husky man's voice spoke.

"No, Sir. I think he was crying?" Another man's voice carries through the door. I rush back to my chair, grimacing while I place my hand behind my back. My heart is pounding as the man walk in the room with a briefcase.

"Luke, how's your shoulder?" The man let out a low laugh.

"It's pretty good considering that it's infected and is creating intensive scar tissue." I give him a fake smile.

The man places his briefcase on the table, then he walks over and picks up the picture of Jacy with a man.

"Did you bring me a present? And it's not even my birthday." I smirk. The man laughs, as he opened the briefcase to reveal a stack of files and a bundle of knives. The man takes out a few files.

"Sort of..." The man picks up one of the files and opens it. He leans against the table silently reading. I moan as a pain shot down my arm and back up into my head. I close my eyes trying not to show pain. "Here's what's going to happen I'm going to ask you a question, if you answer it correctly, you can have a doctor."

"And if I don't?" I raise an eyebrow.

"I will have to make it so that the only way you can get a doctor is if you are almost dead." The man smiles, "ready?"

"Sure, ask away." I smile.

"Let's start off easy, are you affiliated with the organization named The Front?"

"Yes."

"Is it true the man Gabriel Zottigati is the leader of that organization?"

"Yes and no."

"Clarify please," the man squints.

"Yes, he is in charge, but he's not the big boss man," I wink.

"Who is?" I grin as I shrug my shoulders.

"I was never told. All I know is that he is a man in high places." The man scratches his head, thinking of what to say or trying to see if I'm telling the truth or not.

"Moving on, where is The Front's headquarters?"

"The Front constantly moves, from over a million bases across the nation."

"Okay, where is the headquarters now?"

"I don't know," The pain has spread to my chest. My head is pounding and light. My vision begins to blur. I feel a tingling sensation at the tips of my fingers. My body starts to sway, *oh no*.

"Get a medic!" The man shouts as my body collapses to the floor. I hear boots rushing in the room. I moan when they lift me onto a gurney. The lights flicker as they rush me down the hallway into an elevator. I try to count the levels in an effort to keep me lucid, but the pain is overwhelming. The lights dissolve into a darkness.

Jacy, she holds out a hand. I reach my hand into hers. I feel complete as the image dissolves into a flame surrounded by darkness.

Chapter 23

The Flame

When it was my tenth birthday, my brothers turned my house into a homemade theater. They took a white bed sheet and pinned it to the wall. Then they went out and rented a projector. They gave my friends and I two hundred dollars in monopoly dollars, then set up a candy counter just like the movies. I invited my whole class, but only two showed up, Kim and Madison. And ever since that day, they've been my best friends. I miss them. I miss when life was simple... when I didn't have to worry about whether Luke is a villain or a hero. Or if the CIA and the MI6 are corrupt or not. And today is my last day to decide to either trust Gabriel or Thomas. I pace around the room, trying to calm my nerves and loosen my muscles that were still sore from the day Luke and I got separated. I walk around the room, counting my steps, keeping my mind occupied. The room is roughly six feet by seven feet, making it a rectangle. Then I look at the door knob, trying to see if I could pick it. After an hour of staring at the lock, I gave up. So I fiddle with my hair and my clothes, until the door opens.

"Jacy? Are you ready?" Thomas said, his voice is impatient.

"Yes." I rush to the door. My chest fills with excitement. I finally got to leave this room. Thomas's eyes lit up with joy when he sees me leap out the door.

"So, something came up, and Luke had to be transferred to a hospital."

My smile fades. "What happened?" my hands began to shake. My mind wandered to the worst possibility. He could be dead.

"His gunshot wound got infected." Thomas pulls me into a hug, yet somehow he still feels distant. My heart sinks.

"Is he doing better?" My voice cracks as it fills with sadness.

"I don't know... we are going to the hospital." Thomas's voice is oddly comforting.

My heart begins to pound at the thought of seeing Luke. I pull away from Thomas. "I should probably get ready."

Thomas nods. "I'll bring you new clothes and a towel." Thomas escorts me to the showers, then quickly leaves.

Leaving me in the silence of the empty bathroom. I undress slowly seeing the scar on my side from when I out ran the men on the rooftops, and the bruise on my arms, side, and legs from when I went head to head with Thomas's men. I jump in the shower feeling the comforting warmth of the water pour over me. I smile at the first time I finally feel warm in this foreign country. The bathroom fills with steam. When I step out of the shower, there is a towel and my clothes on the counter as well as a note written in the dew on the mirror, 'Meet me in the cafeteria when you're done.' I laugh and shake my head as I gradually put on my clothes. They are different today, I put on a faded, light blue, long sleeve shirt, and my pants are beige, and my shoes are black military boots. I let my sleeves fall to my mid palm. Then, I throw my hair into a high sitting ponytail. Before I leave, as habit I look over my outfit.

I made my way to the dining hall. When I walked in, the tables have been picked up and the kitchen is shut down. Thomas stand by the kitchen talking to a woman. As I draw closer, I watch her hand skim his arm. I rolled my eyes. The girl looked to be around 19 years old. She has a Californian skin tone, that makes her green eyes pop. Her light bronze brown hair flows down to her shoulders. She is tall with an athletic build. On her hip lays her gun and a badge. Once she sees me, her body switches to a defensive position. Her arms fold across her body, her weight shifts to the balls of her feet, ready to strike at any moment.

"Sorry for interrupting," My voice is fake, "Hi, I'm…"

"Jacy, I know." She smiles and returns to Thomas. "I'll talk to you later."

"Okay," Thomas waves as she disappears into the kitchen area.

"She seems nice." My voice is heavy with sarcasm.

"She's not always like that. She just doesn't trust you." Thomas starts towards the hall, I promptly follow.

"Who is she? I see she has a badge. Is she with Interpol?" Thomas's face fill with surprise.

"Yes, she is with Interpol, and her name is Rachel Rose." Thomas smiles, "How did you know she was from Interpol?"

"I'm from America, and my uncle and cousin are international crime lords so that falls under Interpol's jurisdiction." I smile.

Thomas nods.

"I thought the kitchen was supposed to be open every day?" I look back down the hall. There are two men following us. My heart starts to pound.

"Yes, but we are moving to the place we were supposed to go, but you were cold, and Agent Carmichael was here."

Thomas notices the fear rise in my eyes. He looks down the hall.

"Keep walking and play along." Thomas whispers, then threw his body into mine, wrapping his arm around my neck and resting on my shoulders. I wrap one arm around his waist and the other I place on his stomach; my face grows red as my fingers trace the outline of his abs. Thomas laughs, I didn't know whether it is a cover or at me. We stagger down the hall. Every once in a while Thomas would act as if he was whispering into my ear in an effort to see if the men are still following me. "Jacy kiss me." My heart jumps, I shake my head.

"Why?"

"Do it now." I feel his breath on my neck, I turn my head, pressing my lips to his. He staggers back until his back is against the wall. Thomas moves his lips down to my neck, then stops, lifting his lips slightly off my skin, letting his warm breath linger on my neck sending chills down my spine. "They stopped moving, let's move around this corner."

"Okay, who do you think they are?" I said breathless. A smile appears on Thomas's face. He looks down the hall to see how far the corner is.

"I don't know," Thomas nudges my neck with his nose, then falls forward pushing me back into the center of the hallway. We walk around the corner.

"Hello, Jacy, good to see you again." A deep voice said. I tore away from Thomas, straightening out my clothes.

"Hello, Gabriel." My hands begin to shake, my chest feels like a brick is sitting on it.

"Thomas, right?" Gabriel squints with a part smile, Thomas's face is stern. "It's been awhile since I've seen you." I look at Thomas, his face contorts with confusion.

"What?" Thomas said.

"Last time I saw you. It was your first day at the Agency." Gabriel smiles. "Anyways, Jacy. Are you ready?"

Thomas's eyes widen.

I look at Thomas, his eyes wide with part sadness and anger. His face is pleading. I walk over to Gabriel's side.

"Sure, but you have to promise me that you won't hurt Thomas." Gabriel nod, as one of his men take the butt of the gun across his face. I rush over as his body collapses to the floor. "What the hell Gabriel."

"I couldn't have him follow us." His voice is calm. I look at him, my body burns with anger.

"Where are we going?" I toss my hair and roll my eyes. Then begin to follow Gabriel with heavy feet. Gabriel leads me to the elevator and pulls out a gun, my heart pounds, my body wants to run. I want to run.

"We are going to get Luke," Gabriel's cunning smile makes me uneasy. I look at the gun; his eyes follow mine. Gabriel shrugs then lifts the gun towards me, I close my eyes not knowing what he is going to do. "Don't worry I'm not going to shoot you." I open my eyes to see he is handing me the gun. The gun feels heavy in my hand.

"Why do I need this?"

"Because you're the one going in to get him."

"Alone?" My eyes widen in fear, knowing what he is going to say.

"Yes, I got you out, now you have to get Luke out." Gabriel steps out of the elevator and walks to a convoy of vehicles. I follow him to the front vehicle. "I will drop you off at the hospital, you will go in and bring him out using whatever you deem necessary. Okay?" I nod, not really knowing how I will do this. Millions of questions storm my mind. My head pounds as I anticipate the arrival at the hospital. *How am I going to do this?*

Chapter 24

The Raid

The hospital is twelve stories tall, with two guards stationed at the gate. I swallow hard; fear boils up inside me. I look to Gabriel, then back at the doors. I know I have to stay covert as long as I can.

"I need to stay below the radar as long as I can," I sigh knowing one way that I could enter the hospital with no question, but it would be painful.

"What do you have planned?" Gabriel's voice sounds intrigued.

"For me to stay undercover as long as I can, I need to look in pain." I look at him in pain, his face shows no emotion. He nods and steps out of the car, I follow him. I stand with my hands behind my back, Gabriel waits for me to indicate that I'm ready. I don't think anyone is ready to be voluntarily beat up, but I nod. I feel a blinding pain in my eye, my mind is foggy. I feel blood dripping down my cheek, I return to center just as another punch lands on my left jaw. The taste of blood in my mouth making my body shake. I return to center, as Gabriel's foot land in my ribs. I cripple over with pain. All the air is pushed out of my lungs, my chest tightens. I throw up a hand, Gabriel backs off. I look through my hair, to see his eyes, and for the first time they reveal sympathy.

"Ready?" Gabriel helps me up. I nod catching my breath. Am I ready? I have to be. I reach behind my back pulling out the gun Gabriel give me.

"I won't be needing this." I hand the gun to Gabriel.

"Okay," I could tell Gabriel is impressed with my confidence. I smile while bending over to rub dirt all over my face and clothes, to give me a homeless look. Then, I begin to limp towards the doors.

I'm a couple feet from the door when the guards spot me. They pull up their guns, I could see the curiosity fill their eyes. I let out a low moan.

"Halt," one of the guards spoke. His gun shakes and his voice cracks. It must be his first time. I stop throwing a hand into the air.

"Help, please." I plead. The guard walks closer.

"Identify yourself!" The other guard that look as though he has more experience, stayed out of arm's reach.

"My name is Kate. I need a doctor please." I collapse to my knees. The newer guard looks back at the other guard, then backs away, rushing inside. I sit on my knees holding my ribs, trying to think of what I is going to do when I get in there. Soon enough the guard returns with a doctor and a wheelchair. The guards help me into the chair, I groan at every move. They rush me inside to an emergency room. The doctor shines a light in my eyes. I need to find out what room Luke is in. She feels my ribs, I jump as the pain runs through my body. The doctor walks over to the phone that hangs on the wall.

"I'm bringing a seventeen-year-old female up." I smile at the fact she thought I'm seventeen. The doctor walks over to me. "Hello, I am doctor Shell. Nurse Mandie will take you up to X-ray."

"Thank you." I smile. I look at the nurse as she takes me to the elevator. She is short with tight curls in her hair, her skin is pale. Her eyes blue. I shake my head knowing I couldn't pass for her. When we enter the elevator, I immediately look towards the ceiling, there's a possible escape route. I smile as she presses the number 12. "How long do X-rays take?"

"Less than fifteen minutes." I nod, calculating how long it would take for someone to know she was missing and call security. Ten minutes should give me enough time to find Luke, but not guarantee our escape. When we reach the top floor on our way to the X-ray, I count two nurses at the nurses' station. If I could get behind the desk I could see where Luke is. We went to a room just three doors down from the nurse's station. In the room there is a man that stands behind a wall with a Plexiglas window. He is looking down at a chart, when I swing my elbow backwards knocking the nurse in her nose. She staggers backwards, I pop out of the chair slashing my elbow across her face, her body collapse to the floor. I quickly duck and move against the wall.

"What the hell?" the man's voice rings through the intercom. I hear the door open and close. I move to the back side of the door, and as he walks in. I fling my leg striking him across his face, he falls on the ground. I smile not knowing I had that much power in my leg. I quickly grab the man's badge and keys as well as the nurses. As I left, I lock the door and make my way down the hall to the nurses' station. I peek around the corner. There is only one person there now. I stand up straight and limp to the desk.

"Help," I moan. The nurses' eyes widen, and she rushes around the desk to help. I collapse on her, pulling her down to the floor. I quickly slid behind her while wrapping my arm around her neck, and then placing my hand on her mouth. I learned once that if you block blood flow to the brain within five seconds a person would pass out. One, two, three, four, five, and she's out. I release my arm then begin to drag her behind the desk. I quickly rush to the computer, pulling out the ID cards. I swiftly enter in the numbers unlocking the computer. Navigate to the files, and in the search bar I type, Luke Reynold. The room number 204 comes up. My eyes break free of the screen as I hear footsteps approaching. My eyes frantically search the station for something that could possibly disguise me. Then I look at the nurse, she's my height with the same hair color. I rush over to her and pull her into a room across from the nurse's station. I shut the door and rapidly switch our clothes then reappear by the station. I quickly fix my hair into a ponytail and quickly walk to the elevator.

Once I got there I press the button for the second floor. I look at my watch that I borrow from the nurse, I have four minutes left. The door opens to reveal a line of people, I duck my head placing my hand over my bruised face, I walk out towards the rooms, 201, 202, 203. I turn into the next room and rush over to the bed where Luke lays. My eyes swell up, seeing Luke for the first time since he was shot. I look at his shoulder which is bandaged up. He looks peaceful, I place my hand on his chest. Luke's eyes shot open. His hand grabs my arm.

"Luke, it's me. Jacy." His eyes tear up, his lip quivers.

"Jacy?" I nod, Luke reaches his hand cupping my face. I smile grabbing his hand.

"We got to go. Gabriel is waiting outside for us." My voice is soft and caring. Luke nods slowly while he swings his legs over the side of the bed. I help him to his feet. Luke wraps his arm around my shoulders leaning on me. I wrap my arm around his hips. His eyes start to close, "no, Luke you have to stay awake."

"I'll try," We walk out the of the room. I look at my watch I have thirty seconds to get outside. I try to move Luke along, but he keeps drifting in and out of consciousness.

"Code black." The intercom screeches. I look at Luke.

"We have to hurry." Luke nods. I lift him up and pull him into the stairwell. He moans in pain, "I'm sorry but we have to go."

"I can't," Luke whispers as his body starts to fall to the floor.

"No, Luke you need to fight, stay awake please," Luke nods his head and lifting his body back up against mine. We make it to the first floor. I look through the slit in the door and saw the whole floor is swarming with people. I pull Luke closer. "Okay we have to move."

"Okay," Luke pulls me closer as we walk out of the stairwell. We swerve through the crowd. And as we almost make it out the door, the guard spots me. "Hey, stop them!"

I cuss under my breath as I drag Luke outside. The guards rush after us, shots ring through the air. Gabriel's men step out of the truck returning fire, as Luke and I make it to the car. Luke lays across my lap, his eyes shut. I comb the yellow and brown strands of hair out of his face. Then I feel a sharp pain in my shoulder. I take my hand and press it against my shoulder. I brought it into the light, blood. My chest tightens, I'm shot.

Chapter 25

Plan A

It's been sixteen hours since I infiltrated the hospital. Luke has been out since we got in the truck, heading wherever Gabriel is planning on taking us. My arm hurt where the bullet burned my skin. I tear a piece of cloth off the bottom on my shirt and tie it around my arm, slowing down the bleeding. Luke lays on my lap, his eyes close yet dancing. He's dreaming. Water fills my eyes, and a smile appears. I don't know why I'm crying. Maybe because he's safe, or the pain in my arm. I look out the window watching the city lights disappear into the dark scenery. There's no moon tonight; this makes the world feel eerie. My stomach churns, as a bad feeling forms a pit in my chest. I thought back to Thomas. I betrayed him. I betrayed John.

"Miss Jacy, Mr. Gabriel is on the phone for you." The man in the passenger seat leans back and hands me a phone.

"Hello," I whisper trying not to wake Luke.

"Hello Jacy, how is our boy Luke?"

"He's been asleep ever since we left the hospital, and his cheeks are flushed." I study Luke's face.

"Hmm, once we reach base, I will have our doctors take a look at him."

"Thank you... How far are we from base?"

"We are almost there."

"Okay," I studied Luke's face.

"Jacy, we need to talk about Thomas." Gabriel's voice is low. I swallow hard. My heart pounds, and my face grows warm.

"What about him?" I clear my throat. The phone turns to a long beep, "Hello? Gabriel?" I pull the phone away from my ear, connection lost flashes across the screen. I slowly hand it back to the guard. My hands shake. Why would Gabriel need to talk to me about Thomas? I left Thomas; I went with Gabriel. I invaded a hospital with nothing and brought out Luke just as he asked. Why do we need to talk about Thomas? About our kiss? Kisses? I was scared and Thomas told me to kiss him. I take a deep breath trying to slow down my heart rate.

"Jacy?" Luke whispers softly. Excitement stirs in my chest, he's awake.

"Luke, how are you…" I tilt my head as he starts to shake his head. I sink into my seat, he's dreaming.

"Noo, I'll tell… Don't hurt…" Luke's voice cracks. "Stop… Thomas… Please."

My eyes fill with tears. I need to wake him, he needed to know I'm okay.

"Luke, it's me Jacy, I'm safe. You're safe." I comb his hair away from his eyes as they open to reveal the deep blue ocean.

"Jacy?"

I nod, he smiles with tears still in his eyes. Then the smile disappears. His eyes squint remembering his dream or something else.

"What's wrong?" Luke sits up. His face covers with pain. Luke shakes his head.

"Nothing… It's just…" Luke's eyes draw down at his feet.

"Just what?" I scoot closer.

"Nothing." Luke whispers.

"What is it?" Luke shake his head. I attempt making eye contact with him, but his eyes dart away from mine. "Luke." I place both hands on his face.

"It was just a bad dream," he said, tearing his face away from my hands. I lower my eyes, placing my hands in my lap. We sit in silence. I move back over to my side of the truck and occasionally, I would sneak a glance at Luke. He leans his head against the window. His eyes close, and his arm rests across his body. I look back at the window. What did he dream about? Why is he sad? My head pounds with fear. And, on top of that Gabriel wants to talk to me about Thomas. We make our way into a village; the lamp poles lit the streets. The houses are dark, I look at the watch I stole. It was 11:00 pm. I lean back in my seat, closing my eyes. My body relaxes into a deep sleep.

✱✱✱

I didn't know what to say to her. I didn't know how to confront her. So, I pretend to sleep, as pain shots down my arm. I peek over at Jacy, her body relaxes, her breath is steady.

"Toby," I said quietly. The man in the passenger seat turn to face me. "Where are we?"

"We are just outside of Northampton, about five hours away from base." He nods.

"Thank you, can you get Gabriel on the phone?" Toby nods, reaching into his pocket then handing me a phone.

"Hello?" Gabriel's voice crackled through the phone.

"This is Luke."

"Luke, how are you feeling?"

"I need our doctors to look at my arm. They removed all the infected tissue, but it needs clean bandages."

"That can be arranged."

"Also can you tell me about how you got Jacy?"

"Yes, she was with Thomas and I used my ID to get in, while Jessica took out the security system. And my men followed Thomas and Jacy in the hallway and once she made us I appeared, and, long story short, I took Jacy to get you out and…"

"Wait, Jacy got me out?"

"Yes, don't you remember?" Gabriel's voice grows concerned.

"I had just gotten out of surgery. I don't remember anything."

"Oh, well, Jacy went in unarmed and brought you out."

"By herself?"

"Yes." I look over at her. She risked her life for me. A warm feeling appears in my chest, and a smile grows on my face. *Thank you.*

"Luke?"

"I'm here." I move closer to Jacy.

"I have some bad news for you."

"And that is?"

"Jacy has to go back with Thomas."

Tessa L. Gatz

"Why?" My voice deepens, the warmth disappears.

"I need her to keep an eye over there, and now that I know I can trust her, she will keep me in the loop so that I won't get caught before I finish what they call Project Maverick, and then I can return to the agency."

"Why can't Jessica do it?" I shrug.

"Because, Thomas has a thing for Jacy."

I growl and roll my eyes. Of course, he does. Who wouldn't? She's intelligent, strong, and beautiful? "Listen, Luke, I have to go, but I know you don't like this but it's what we need. I'll talk to you later."

"Bye," I hand the phone back to Toby. I just got you back and now you have to leave again. I wrap my arm around her pulling her into my chest, synchronizing our breaths... inhale... exhale. I close my eyes, resting my head on her. I drift off into a world of imagination where there are no more spies, no more lies, and no more secrets.

186

Chapter 26

The News

It's black, my arms are strapped to the chair. Two men stand in front of me. Their faces hidden by masks. The men circle me like lions. My heart races as one of the men stops and leans in. I feel a sense of security. His lips gently touch mine, tears begin to run down my face, as a gunshot rings. The man in front of me fell to the ground. I look behind me at the other man, holding a gun. I look back at the man on the ground his mask has fallen off, to reveal Luke. My heart drops. I slowly look behind me to see the man as his mask disappears, John.

The truck stops throwing my body forward, Luke's grip tighten around my body. I wince at the pain in my arm and side. My face is swollen from yesterday.

"Good, morning princess," Luke smirk, leaning in and placing a gentle kiss on my cheek. My face grows red as I turn to face him. His eyes look down at my arm where dark red blood drips.

"It's just a scratch." I smile, placing my palm on his jaw and having my fingers slide into his hair, that has grown since the last time I saw him.

"It looks a little more than a scratch. I'll have the doctor check it out." Luke's smile is comforting. I miss him.

"How is your wound?" Luke winces as he shrugs.

"It's pretty good." My eyes studied his eyes. They were filled with pain and questions.

"Luke, Jacy, We are here," The driver said, stepping out of the truck then opening mine. I slide out of the truck into a gravel driveway that's leading to a small cottage, with aged stone and honeysuckle vines running up the wall to a window. There was a stone fence that framed the yard. Luke's fingers lace perfectly into mine while his other arm is slung across his body with a piece of fabric. I stand in awe of how beautiful it is. A smile appears on my face as Luke pulls me towards the new place that I will call home for now. Luke leads me through the door that reveals a magnificent common area. The warm wood floors pairs nicely with the modern art on one wall and a white half circle couch that faces a TV on the other wall just above a gas fireplace. It looks to have two bedrooms, with one bath and a small kitchen. I analyzing every detail while Luke guides me through the house, the glass doors leading to a porch that faces a meadow filled with flowers and sheep. The stairwell spirals to a floor that holds two bedrooms. I spin around taking in all the beauty. The rooms have king-sized beds with a wooden-frame side tables, the floor has a white rug that is framed by the corners with two chairs and a coffee table. Each room is connected to a bathroom. The floor is a white tile that matches the grey walls and pairs with the wooden cupboards. The counter is a dark marble that holds a sink.

I walk into the bedroom, and with one leap, I land on the bed. My body aches, but the feeling of a soft and comfortable place to sleep made it ache a little less. Luke makes his way over to me. A laugh escapes my mouth. I realize this is the first time I didn't care what happens next, all I care about is that I get to sleep in a warm comfortable bed. Luke flops beside me studying the ceiling. A smile grew on his face when he caught me staring at him.

"What?" Luke said with a laugh.

"Nothing, just looking around."

"In one direction?" Luke looks at me with a smile that makes me forget about everything. About the gun shot, about the fact I left Thomas and my brother. About Gabriel, Jessica and Uncle Larry.

"Yes, but I might have to switch because it's not the prettiest." I smirk turning away from him. Then I feel the warmth of his chest press against my back, and his breath on my neck. A shiver shoots down my spine, I roll my eyes hoping he didn't feel it.

"Are you cold?"

Not anymore I thought as I shake my head. Luke moves his hand towards my face, gently moving my hair off my neck.

"Jacy..." Luke's eyes pause on my lips.

"Guys..." Jessica walks in, the air fills with tension as she quickly turns around and places a hand on her head. "Sorry to barge in but Gabriel would like to talk to both of you."

"We will be right down." My voice low. Jessica promptly left the room leaving the door open. I look at Luke then slowly make our way downstairs.

Gabriel sits on the couch with Jessica. They hold glasses of what looks like champagne. Jessica is staring into her glass. Her eyes hold anger and sadness. I sit beside Gabriel while Luke stands by the fireplace. Jessica's eyes bounce between Luke and me. My eyes avoid hers, while Luke's stay fixed on me.

"First, I would like to welcome Luke back, and thank Jacy for bringing him back safely." Gabriel said as he claps his hands, while Jessica forces a smile. "And let's not forget how Jessica made sure everyone was in place." I nod making sure I keep my eyes focused on my shoes.

"Let's talk about phase two." Jessica's voice is prompt and stern.

"Phase two?" I said looking at Luke, who shrugs.

"Yes, Jacy this phase is all on you. You have to go back to Thomas and keep an eye on the operation from there as Luke, Jessica and I initiate phase three." Gabriel smiles, "Phase three is where Luke, Jessica and I will have you bring Thomas and your brother to a secret location where your Uncle's shipment will be coming in."

"When and where is this supposed to go down?" That's the first sentence where Luke has showed any interest in the topic. I watch a sigh escape his lips, and his eyes narrow.

"Those details will be revealed later, but first, we need to focus on getting Jacy ready to go back with Thomas." Gabriel motions towards me. I look at Luke whose eyes show no emotion.

"What do I need to know?" I said, my voice fill with anger, as my chest tightens, at the thought that *Luke doesn't care about me.*

"You need a cover story for why you are back, and you need to know everything about Thomas. Because you need to get close to him, and you need him to trust you." Gabriel nods at Jessica as she tosses a file across the table. As I pick it up, I look at Luke who still shows no emotion. I scold myself for caring about him. Why doesn't he care?

"I need to read all of this?" Gabriel nods and eases back into his seat, crossing his legs.

"Also, there will be another person with you on the inside. She will be your direct handler, and if you have any questions ask her, and she will tell you when and what to do."

"Who is it?" I look towards the kitchen as a woman appears. I squint trying to remember where I know her from.

"Hello Jacy, it's nice to see you." Agent Rose smiles.

"Agent Rose is it?" My eyes follow her.

She nods as she walks over and squeezes between Gabriel and me. I roll my eyes then begin to go stand by Luke when Jessica clears her throat. I look at her and move to the other side of the fireplace, in hope that would be a neutral territory.

"So, I will be your liaison. If you need anything, come to me. I will give you the details on when phase three begins and how to get to phase three." I nod and glance at Luke as he rests against the wall. Really, he doesn't care. I'm going back to Thomas, and he doesn't even blink.

"What happens once we are done?" Luke said, his voice monotone.

"Then we return back to our normal lives." Jessica said.

"What happens if the plan fails?" I said looking around the room. Everyone's eyes draw downwards, and a bad feeling starts to rise in my gut.

"Then people die." Gabriel's voice is filled with sorrow.

"Well, then we can't fail." I smile, opening the file, scanning the pictures, and case reports.

"Okay, Jacy get caught up. Luke, and Jessica I need to talk to you. Agent Rose, you need to go back to Thomas." Everyone disperses to their assigned area; I walk upstairs. Then stop at the top backing away from the railing, far enough where Jessica, the furthest away, couldn't see me.

"Jessica, you and Luke will go down to the market tomorrow and get supplies to set up the rally point, while I get Jacy prepared for her story before we tip off the SIS about this house." Luke and Jessica nod.

"How close does Jacy have to get to Thomas, because I don't trust him." Luke's voice is clear, and authoritative.

"As close as she can," Gabriel said, "I know you don't like it, but this is what she needs to do. Now, back to business. You need to go to the bar tonight. There is someone there that will bring a folder with confidential intel in it. Once you acquire it bring it back to me. Now go."

"Yes, sir." They say as they left the room. I turn and walk towards the same room Luke and I were in earlier. I sit in the chair next to the fireplace, reviewing the file. *This better work.*

Chapter 27

Phase Two

I find myself spending most of the night wading through the files on Thomas. All of his clandestine operation in Africa, Algeria, Terickistan, Bolivia, and Nigeria. The file is thick with photos of him dressed in street clothes talking to men or women. One shows Thomas in a long-sleeve shirt and cargo pants with knee patches with a scarf that covers the lower half of his face. It looks as though he was talking to a woman. All I could see of her is her eyes. The picture is a grainy black and white. In the bottom right corner, it said 10/35 PRCP, I stare at the letters trying to find out what they meant.

After a while I give up and move on to the files. Reading them is like reading a book with the all the exciting parts blacked out with a sharpie. It read over the first file twice looking for any detail that could help get to Thomas on a personal level, to coerce him into trusting me. I still wasn't sure about Gabriel's plan, the way he needs Thomas to go to a certain place at a certain time. It seems shady. But Gabriel is shady and so is Uncle Larry. And if I am going find out anything, I need to go with Gabriels plan. Even if I didn't agree with it.

It's around three in the morning when I hear Luke and Jessica return from their mission at the bar. I'm suddenly alert, and I slid out of bed. The feeling of the cool floor against my bare feet sends chills up my spine. I slowly walk to the door opening it slightly. I peek through the slit, looking for them. I listen intently as their footsteps grow closer and their voices louder.

"Luke can I ask you a question?" Jessica's voice is soft.

"Is it about tonight and the mission?" My heart flutters at the sound of Luke's voice as it, too, is soft.

"No, it's about you... and Jacy."

"What about us?"

"Do you trust her?"

"Oddly yes. When I was first given the task to get into her friend group, I thought she would be a spoiled brat, considering who her Uncle is but, she turned out to be the smartest person in the room, and the kindest. Also, she broke me out of a hospital and gave me a run for my money when I trained her." His voice is warm and filled with emotion.

"Hmm I don't see that. I see her as a kid who doesn't know how to take care of herself and is going to get us into trouble, and possibly get us killed."

"She's been lied to her whole life, and now the truth is pouring out through her dangerous Uncle and her brother."

"Still, I don't trust her." Jessica said coldly.

"Just give her time she will impress you." Luke said defensively.

"I guess we will see." Jessica snarks. I roll my eyes. A pain shot up my arm, and I wince in pain, falling forward against the door. I curse as the door squeales.

"Jacy?" Luke's voice changes back to soft as he walks over to the door. I scoot away as he opens it to see me on the floor. "What are you doing up?"

"You know just pleasure reading." I point at the files that cover my bed. His eyes search mine. A smile appears on his face. I roll my eyes reaching my hand towards him as an indicator to help me up. His large hand wraps around mine lifting me to my feet. Luke's hand lingers on mine. I hate how he had a power over me: the way his smile makes my face grow red, while his touch made my arms grow goosebumps, and how his eyes are like the ocean, so much that still needs to be uncovered.

"Am I interrupting?" Luke jumps at the sound of Jessica's voice. He steps away, placing his hand on the back of his neck. I cross my arms. Why is he hiding me? I hate to admit it but I hated how Luke always withdrew when Jessica shows up.

"Nope," my voice is like a frozen tundra of hatred. I search her up and down as Luke just stands in the corner waiting. What was he waiting for? His hand is shaking, he must be nervous. Why is he nervous? Our eyes connected; I tilt my head trying to read his mind.

"Luke, are you coming?" Jessica turns towards the door. Luke's eyes never left mine.

"No, I'm going to stay here and help Jacy with the files." Luke said with a smile. Jessica nods and left just as quickly as she came. I follow Luke to the bed where the files are scattered in a fan-shaped mess on the bed.

"You can go with Jessica, if you want. You don't need to help me with these files." Luke smiles moving papers, making room for him to sit. I did the same thing.

"I want to help." My heart leaps, at the thought of Luke wanting to stay with me. I smile and look through the files again.

I didn't know when I had fallen asleep. It must have been around five in the morning, or four. Luke and I searched through each file, looking for Thomas's mistakes and a weakness so that my cover would appeal towards his sensitive side. Luke told me that this would bring him closer to trusting me. I'm not sure if Thomas would trust me no matter what cover I put on. He saw me walk away from him; he saw me walk over to Gabriel. I know if I was him I wouldn't trust me. When I wake up my head lays heavy on Luke's chest, my arm is stretched across his stomach. I could hear the soothing sound of the air filling his lungs as he inhales. I wish I could stay here, where all my problems seem to melt away. I open my eyes to a picture of Thomas, and I know that it would be impossible for me to stay here. I slowly slip out of bed, leaving Luke asleep peacefully as I make my way down stairs.

"Good morning Jacy. How was the reading assignment?" Jessica smiles. She's sitting at the bar with a bowl in front of her, and to her right sits Gabriel. His eyes smile a smile of suspicion, which always makes me question if I could trust him.

"It was good. I learned that Thomas as a young child had a father that was abusive to him and his mother. Also, he has a brother and a sister, and every Sunday he goes to church with them." I inform Gabriel.

"So what's your plan for gaining his trust?" Gabriel's look said he already knew what I'm about to say.

"I am going to tell a sad story about my past. He will sympathize with me and hopefully make him feel like he needs to protect me." I smile, knowing that it's a good plan. Gabriel nods slightly.

"Good. So tonight we will begin phase two." He gets up and walks over to me, and placing his hand between my shoulder blades, guiding me to a room in the back just past the kitchen. "Here is where Thomas will find you."

"So I will look like a prisoner." Gabriel nods. The room is dark and gloomy with a single light hanging from the ceiling over a metal chair, that has handcuffs welded onto the arms of the chair.

"Yes." I look behind me to see Luke standing in the doorway, his face fills with disgust. He didn't like the plan. And now neither did I.

✳✳✳

Sixteen hundred hours, at the SIS moving headquarter. Thomas and John have been working frantically to find where Jacy was taken. They went over the video feeds of a girl breaking into their hospital, to break out one guy. The girl takes out six nurses and got past multiple armed guards to escape into a convoy of black sedans with no license plates. Thomas has a cut on his head where Gabriel's men had slammed his face with the gun.

"You boys look mad." Agent Rose walks into the room. John rolls his eyes; you could tell he wasn't in the mood for her mouth today.

"Well when you lose an asset and my sister in one night I tend to get a little irritated." John's voice is low and intense with anger. Thomas walks over to the computer playing the surveillance footage back, looking at each frame as though there is a hidden meaning behind each move.

"I see. Well if you didn't put the boy into so much pain where he would collapse maybe they both would be here right now." Agent Rose snaps at John. His eyes widen.

"Guys!" Thomas yells, as he points at the footage. John and agent Rose walk over looking closer, and in the corner of the screen there is a woman. Thomas enhances the video, the picture is grainy but still decipherable, "I know where they are." Thomas jumps out of his chair, John and Agent Rose follow him to a car outside their mobile facility.

"Who was that?" John said towards Thomas as he jumps into the driver's seat.

"That's Jessica," John looks at Thomas, confusion covers his face. "She's working for Gabriel."

Chapter 28

Camera, Lights, Action

The darkness swallows me as I run through the trees into a field of tall grass that stings my skin. I can't breathe, but I can't stop either. I didn't know who I is running from, all I know is that I can't get caught. The grass blocks my view, I don't know where I'm going. I glance back to see lights moving through the grass behind me. My heart is pounding in my ears. My lungs burn. *I need to get away. I need to escape.* I keep running faster and faster, until the tall grass gives way to a man. He is tall, his dark hair floats in the wind. His eyes are a light brown. And in his hand, he holds a gun. I close my eyes, dropping to my knees. A deafening sound ring around me.

"Jacy, wake up. It's time." Luke gently shakes my shoulder. I look at Luke, I know he could tell that I'm scared. I could see it in his eyes. He is scared too. My hands shake,

Luke wraps his hands around mine. They are warm, a breath of relief leaves my lungs. He helps me to my feet, then pulls me into a hug. "Everything will be alright. I will be watching everything." Luke whispers, I pull back just enough for our eyes to meet. We stay there for a minute taking in this last moment before I will leave for... I don't even know how long I will be gone. Luke leans in, laying a gentle kiss on my lips.

"Jacy time to go." A voice sounds, Luke and I break apart. As I walk toward the room, fear arises in my heart. I can't do this, I have to. I have no choice. I sit in the chair; Gabriel walks over to me securing the handcuff to my wrists. "We will be watching every move." I nod, as they left shutting the door, leaving me in the darkness...

✳✳✳

Thomas, John, and Agent Rose arrives at the cottage two hours after Gabriel left leaving Jacy in a cold dark room. The team barges into the cottage, blowing the door off the hinges. Thomas and Agent Rose sweep the top floor while John and another agent clear the lower floor. John runs into two guards, one by the back-sliding glass doors. John lets off two shots, one passes through the guard's shoulder the other through his leg. The agent walks over to the guard taking his gun away, while keeping his own gun trained on the guard.

After the agent gave John the go ahead, he peaks around the corner, to see the second guard asleep in front of a door. John stealthily walks over to the man, and takes a syringe filled with a bright blue liquid out of his pocket. The guard's eyes open as John's hand cover the guard's mouth and inserts the needle into his neck. The guard's eyes closed as his body goes limp.

"John the upstairs is clear." Thomas said, walking towards the door. Agent Rose followed closely behind him.

"Something's not right, there're only two guards." John's voice is full of question.

"Only two?" Agent Rose repeats.

"Yes," John nods.

"What's behind the door?" Thomas reach out jiggling the doorknob.

"I don't know," John scans the room, as though looking for someone else.

"What are you looking for?" Thomas said, scanning the room as well.

"I don't know." John's voice lowers to a whisper.

"Well, the door is locked." Thomas said, "Rachel, do you have a lock pick set?"

"Yes," Agent Rose pulls out two thin silver sticks with hooks on the end. She kneels and starts to work while John walks back to the first guard, looking back outside the glass doors. A red dot appears, moving to the left side of his chest.

"John get down!" Thomas yells. John looks back at Thomas who is rushing toward him. The bullet shatters the glass, just as Thomas leaps, knocking John to the ground. Then, a hail of gunfire makes the room explode.

"Are you okay?" John asks Thomas.

"Yes, are you?" Thomas looks around the room.

"Yes," John said as he watches Thomas crawl over to a desk. The gunfire has stopped which left an eerie feeling of stillness in the air.

"John, Thomas are you okay?" Agent Rose yells.

"We are okay. There's a sniper on the south side." Thomas yells as he knocks down the table then pulls it over to John.

"What are we going to do with this?" John said.

"We are going to use it as cover." Thomas smiles.

"You think this table can protect us from a high-powered rifle?"

"No, but if we push it into the doorway, it might trick the sniper into shooting it. When he changes his clip, we will rush over to the counter." John nods, seeing that it sounds like a good idea.

"Okay," John says, and Thomas heaves the table in front of the doors. Three shot breaks through the wood. Thomas counts to three, then crawls across the floor.

"Now your turn." Thomas waves John across, he quickly crawls.

"Thomas, John, I think you need to see this." Agent Rose said. Thomas tilts his head and walks over by Agent Rose. His eyes water, and his heart aches, as he sees Jacy strapped to a chair with a bruised face and a bloody arm. Her head hangs, her lips are dry and cracked.

"Jacy..." Thomas rushes over, lifting her head. Her hair is tangled and damp with sweat. Jacy moans a little.

"Thomas?" Her voice is hoarse.

"Jacy!" John yells, rushing over and pushing Thomas out of the way. "What did they do?" His eyes fill with anger.

"John?" Her eyes flutter open and close as though a weight is holding them down.

"Jacy, we are going to get you out of here okay." Thomas says, looking back at Agent Rose who stands in the doorway, shocked. "Agent Rose, come here and unlock her."

"Oh yeah, sorry." Agent Rose rushes over to Jacy, "Thomas get John out of here."

Thomas nods taking John out of the room.

"Thomas?" Jacy repeats in a low voice.

"No, it's me Agent Rose." she whispers, "what happened?"

"This is from when I had to rescue Luke," Jacy whispers, "my arm needs medical attention."

"Don't worry. We will take care of it," Agent Rose says, as she releases both of Jacy's hands, then pull a syringe out of her pants pocket. "This will put you to sleep." She injects it into Jacy's neck.

"The medical transport is here." Thomas says to Agent Rose, as the EMT's came in with a gurney. They lift Jacy onto the gurney and escort her to the truck. "You go with John, and I'll go with Jacy." Thomas said to Agent Rose. She nods and jumps into the car with John, while Thomas jumps into the ambulance. As the truck took off, Thomas's hand covers Jacy's. And he whispers, "you can't leave yet, your family needs you. I need you."

Chapter 29

The Factory

My head pounds, as I slowly open my eyes. I'm lying in a bed with what looks and feels like an off-white cotton sheet. The room is cream with white tiles. There is a window that shows a dark grey sky. There's a single IV in my arm that led to a bag full of a candy red liquid. I didn't know how long I'd been out, but I feel refreshed, as though I could run a marathon. Although I feel fine, I couldn't help but thinking something is missing. The pain. I look at my arm, there's a clean bandage covering the wound. I move my arm around, smiling at the fact that I could finally move it.

"Hello Miss Kasy, how are you feeling?" A nurse walks in carrying a tray, that contains jello, with a yellow cup and a blue straw.

"Better, how long was I out?" I say clearing my throat.

"A day." My heart drops, I shake my head in disbelief. I couldn't be out for a day. I pinch the bridge of my nose trying to recall what has happened. All I remember is one of Gabriel's men giving me a shot, then after that nothing.

"Where am I?" I look out the window again.

"You're still in the England." My heart fluttered at the sound of his thick accent.

"Thomas," my cheeks turn a light pink, as I turn to see him standing in the doorway. His smile reminds me of home.

"How are you feeling?" His voice is soft with a hint of urgency as if we are running out of time.

"I feel better." I turn to see him, still handsome and powerful.

"I need to ask you some questions," Thomas pulls out a notebook and a pen. I already know what he's going to ask. Why did you go with Gabriel? Are you working with them? What is their plan? My stomach stirs, I didn't know how much to tell, or if I should say anything at all. Then a woman walks in, a shiny badge on her hip with a black beauty holstered beside it.

"Thomas, is she ready?" Agent Rose says with a smile.

"No, but she will in a few seconds," Thomas's smile turns stern as Agent Rose left the room.

"What's going on?" confusion fills my mind.

"I have some question, that I don't want her to hear," Thomas said, pulling a chair over to the side of my bed.

"Okay, what kind of questions?" Fear fills my body, I didn't know why I'm scared I had prepared for this, I read his file.

"Like, why did you help Gabriel break out Luke Reynolds from one of our hospitals?"

"Because I needed to know if he was okay."

"I see," Thomas's eyes are cold with disbelief, I need him to trust me. "Is that why you left with Gabriel or was it for something bigger?"

"What do you mean?"

"Like money, love, drugs. Family?" His voice is condescending.

"When I left, I didn't know what he had planned, but I knew Luke would either be with him, or he would get him."

"Did you know Jessica was a part of The Fronts organization?"

"No," My palms are sweaty now, and my hands are shaking. But with every question Thomas asks, I feel like he is asking something else.

"Okay that's all," I could tell Thomas is lying. There's another question he wasn't asking. Just as I'm about to ask him what he really wanted to know Agent Rose walks in.

"Ready?" Agent Rose said.

"Yes," Thomas nods.

"Jacy, how did you get involved with Gabriel." Agent Rose said to me with a smile.

"He saved me from some men who were chasing me." I smile.

"Is Jessica involved with Gabriel?"

"Yes."

"How long did you know that Jessica is involved with him?"

"Only after I rescued Luke." I look at Thomas who is standing in the corner now, while Agent Rose interrogates me. His face turns red, a light red and his eyes narrow in what I would describe as disgust, when I said Luke's name. is he jealous?

"Why did you rescue Luke?" Agent Rose said while giving me a small nod, telling me to continue.

"He saved me, too many times, and he was… my friend."

"Was?" Agent Rose said. I look at Thomas, his stance changed. He leans forward, off the wall, showing more interest now.

"Yes, was. Once I rescued him, they turned on me, handcuffing me to a chair, interrogating me."

"What did they ask you?"

"They asked me about Thomas and my brother, and about your operations," I said, Agent Rose gives me a smile, knowing that I did well. Yet I feel bad that I lied. I lied to Thomas.

"What did you tell them?" Thomas jumped in.

"Nothing, but they had files. Stacks of them."

"Did you get to see them?" Thomas walks closer to me, asking each question faster and faster.

"No,"

"So, for all you know these files could be on their own agents."

"Yes," my heart is racing.

"For all we know you could be lying about all of this," my eyes water as Thomas raised his voice, shaking the room.

"Why would I lie?"

"Why would you?" A tension fills the room that left an uncomfortable feeling hanging in air. I stare into Thomas's eyes, building the tension of anger, and jealousy.

"I'm not lying." My voice was low, my eyes never waver from his.

"I think that will be all for now." Agent Rose said, her voice cracks with an awkward sound. Thomas's eyes break free, as he turns to follow Agent Rose out of the room.

It isn't long before some of their men came in and take me to a truck. I'd been in the truck for around two hours. Throughout that time I thought of the earlier conversation, with Thomas, and Agent Rose. I didn't know whether to feel insulted or honored. Insulted because he thought that I had lied to him, even though I did, or honored because he's jealous of Luke. The more I think about it the more I realize it didn't matter. The truck came to a stop. I wait as Thomas's men to open the door to reveal a small, base camp with rows of green tents and a single building that has a sign that said, 'Camp Hamilton.' The men place handcuffs on me as they escort me into a tent that has a single cot and a wood stove. The men uncuff me then stand by the door, waiting.

"Jacy," I crinkle my nose knowing all too well whose voice that belongs to.

"John, I thought you left." My voice is cold.

"I did. But once I heard that you had been taken again, I came back to help you."

"Sure, you came back to help me. Just admit it you would rather be on your mission then seeing if I'm okay."

"That's not true, I came back to find you and I left for you and for the family."

"No, you left for yourself, not for me. Not for our family. Only for you!" My veins boiled with anger.

"Is that what you think?" John's eyes fill with hurt.

"Why else would you get me back, then leave me with a stranger. Then not even care about what I did or had to do."

"I see," John looks at the ground. I didn't know what to say, he left me. Now I see what Josh was talking about. John only thinks about himself and no one else.

"Tell me I'm wrong." My voice is challenging.

He turns and leaves. My heart sinks. I want to be wrong, I want him to tell me I'm wrong. I couldn't fight it anymore. All my emotion explodes like a volcano, and I collapse on the cot as tears roll down my face. I cry until my eyes grow dry and a headache forms. And I thought, *I can't do this anymore. I want to go home.*

Chapter 30

The Bond

The fight weighs on my mind through the night. I didn't understand why he left. Was it really for me? Or was it for an advancement in his career? Or was it to just complete his mission? I'm not sure if I care anymore. All I know is I want this to end. I want to go back where all I had to worry about was if I could meet my friends on Saturday. I wonder what Kim and Madison are doing. I haven't had any contact with them since the day I was taken to Russia. Now that seems like forever ago. I try to count back weeks I've been gone. I estimate about three five weeks. Did they know I'm gone? Most likely not.

"Jacy, can we talk?" I look over to see John standing in the doorway. I want to say no, partly because I'm still mad, and because I don't want to fight anymore.

"Sure," I said, as he gingerly walks into the tent.

"I'm sorry I made you feel like I abandoned you." I study his face looking to see if he's being sincere. "I didn't mean for you to feel that way."

"Then stop hiding things and stop walking away." I said.

"That's why I came here, to tell you everything." John smiles, as he sits down by the wood stove in the corner.

"Okay," my voice fills with disbelief.

"As you already know, I'm a CIA agent. I've been an agent since my sophomore year in college. And when I got to the agency, they sent me on a few field assignments that led me to the mission I am working on today. The same mission that I left for, for five months." John pauses, seeing if I'm following. "The mission was called Project Maverick. I spent those five months undercover in Russia, London, Spain, and Africa, doing operations for a man who I believed was the head of the operations. So I ran an operation that failed. After that the agency sent me home."

"So you failed your mission."

John nods."Once I arrived home, I was supposed to take those days to recuperate, but then you said Gabriel was there. So I contacted my agency and took Mama June, and Josh to the safe house, and contacted Grandma Gin, but you were just so stubborn you wouldn't come with me, and that's when you got taken. So I followed you to London. Where I made a deal with the SIS."

"John your time is up." One of the guards in the corner said.

"Okay, can you just give me another minute?" The guard checks his watch, then nods. "The deal was that they would help me get you back safely and I would complete Project Maverick for them, considering I had a cover ID already set up and I was already in the organization."

"So that's why you left, to complete a mission you already failed at?" John nods.

"Once I saw you, I didn't truly leave, though. That boy that you saved, I was talking to him."

"Luke? You were the one that was talking to him?" I take deep breaths trying to keep my anger down.

"Yes, he's involved with The Front." John looks at his watch then stands up. "Jacy I have to go."

"Where?" I stand up and walk towards him. The guards raise their guns. I feel like a criminal.

"I need to go finish my mission." A guilty feeling arises in my chest. I know it's because I know about Gabriel. I know his plan, but I need Thomas to trust me first. Maybe if I tell John he could convince Thomas, and I know Agent Rose will play along. But is it worth the risk? "Jacy?"

"Can you bring Thomas in here? I need to talk to him." I smile, stepping back from John allowing the guards to lower their guns. John nods then quickly exits the tent. I didn't know why I ask for Thomas. Panic starts to rise in my chest. I scold myself. *Why would you do that? What are you going to say? What are you going to do?*

"Jacy? You called for me?" Thomas walks in and I freeze. I didn't understand his effect on me. It's overpowering. I nod, walking over to the wood stove, while tracking him with my eyes, as he follows in my direction. "What did you want to talk about?"

"About The Front." I smile, studying his eyes.

"What about it?" Thomas smiles placing his hands in his pockets.

"About your plan to take it down."

"That's confidential," Thomas smiles.

"I know, but so am I, right?" I smile flirtatiously.

"Why did you really call me in here?" I look at the guards. Thomas traced my eyes and nodded at the guards to go outside. "Okay they're gone. Now will you tell me?"

"I don't trust Agent Rose." *Really? That's what you came up with?* I scolded myself.

"Why not?" Thomas squints, and I could see the suspicion rising in his eyes.

"Because she's working with Gabriel," Thomas nods his head. He already knows that.

"I know, but she will lead us to Gabriel."

"How did you know?"

"She left the same day you did. Then returned a day before we led a raid on the house where we found you. Also, when we were searching upstairs, she knew the floor plan too well."

"I see, what's your plan with her?" The fire is getting too warm, I walk towards Thomas.

"Use her to bring us to Gabriel." Thomas takes his hands out of his pockets, as if I make him nervous.

"What are your plans with me?" I don't know how to execute Gabriel's plan now. I didn't know what to do. Maybe I could help Thomas and my brother then convince them to give Luke immunity.

"I don't know yet." Thomas takes a step back.

"Let me help," Thomas shakes his head.

"No, it's too dangerous." I smile at the thought of him protecting me. Or at least trying to.

"I've been in more danger. I spent a month with Gabriel a man who kidnapped me and runs an international crime ring, and I lived with my Uncle who apparently does the same."

"Wait, your Uncle?" Thomas's eyes widen.

"Yes, he is who Gabriel is going after. Gabriel says…" I stop, realizing what I'm about to say, I couldn't say it. It would ruin Gabriel's operation, unless Gabriel is lying. Then it wouldn't matter.

"Gabriel said what?" Thomas walks closer; his voice is low. I feel a strange feeling that I should tell him, that I need to tell him.

"He said he's with the SIS. He spent ten years undercover trying to get into my Uncle's organization to take him down. He told me that the operation was off the books, so his records were scrubbed from the system." Thomas stands looking at me for what feels like an hour.

"Come with me." Without waiting for my response, he grabs my hand pulling me out into the brisk air. "I'm taking her with me, if anyone asks, she's asleep." Thomas said to the guards. Before they could even acknowledge the order, Thomas rushes me behind the tents, keeping me out of sight.

"Where are you taking me?" I said breathless while we continue stalking behind the tents.

"We are going into the building."

"Why?"

"I'll show you once we get in there," Thomas's voice is lathered with annoyance. I constantly scan my surroundings as Thomas drags me to the last tent before it opens to enter the building. I run into his shoulder; he turns with a half smirk. "We need to disguise you. Wait here."

I nod, while he walks around the corner.

It's been five minutes since Thomas disappeared. I thought about leaving, but if I left then Thomas wouldn't trust me. It's the simple things that can break trust. My heart flutters when I heard footsteps approaching. I look to see it isn't Thomas. My heart sinks, as I quickly turn around having my back face the woman.

"Hello? Who are you?" She said. Her voice is shaky. I listen and wait for her footsteps to grow closer. My heart pounds as I hear the metal of the gun move in her hand. I know I have to wait until she is right next to me before I could make my move. "Identify yourself."

Her voice carries more authority now. Her footsteps are heavy, as the gravel cracks under her unbalanced weight. Three. Two. One. I pull my shirt over my face, so that only my eyes peeking over the hem. Then I swing my leg back kicking her in the top right shoulder. You could hear her ribs crack as well as her clavicle. She drops her gun as she fell down to the ground. I grab the gun then whipped it across her face. Her eyes close, and her body goes limp. I stand there holding the gun looking at her when Thomas walks around the corner.

"Good it worked." Thomas said as he walks over to me.

"What worked." I said. My face contorts with confusion.

"This is your disguise." Thomas points at the girl laying on the ground. I look at him then her. I roll my eyes and start to swap clothes.

"Excuse me," I look at Thomas.

"I'll keep a lookout," he smiles, and turns around. I roll my eyes and finish switching clothes. I walk over to Thomas, and gently place my hand on his shoulder. He jumps, and his face turns red. "Ready?"

"Yes," Thomas grabs my hand and pulls me out into the opening. I have on a camo uniform with a black cap that I pull down over my eyes. As we enter the building Thomas let go of my hand. The building has elegant white walls with old wooden floors, and two staircases on either side of the room that leads to the second floor. Thomas leads me to a room behind the staircase on the far-left side of the room. The room is filled with books and boxes. "What is this place?"

"This is the burn room," Thomas shut the door behind me and locked it. "It's all the files of all the covert agents we have, and have had, dating back ten years. So, if Gabriel really was a spy, then his paper file will be in here." Thomas opens his arms as though inviting the challenge.

"But he said his record was scrubbed."

"Yes, but we always have copies of copies." Thomas walks up behind me placing his hand on my shoulder guiding me to a shelf. "You start here. This is all the G's and Z's"

"Okay," I grab a box and haul it to the table, and Thomas did the same. We repeat this for about an hour until all the boxes are around that one table. Thomas grabs a seat as did I, and a file.

I spend five hours going through the G's while Thomas went through the Z's. Every once in a while, I would catch Thomas looking at me. My stomach would turn with butterflies, just thinking of him. I'm not sure why I feel such a strong connection with him. But I did, more than I felt with Luke.

"I found something." Thomas smiles, moving over to my side of the table, placing the folder in front of me. For some reason I'm very aware of his body hovering over me. "Look here." Thomas points at a picture.

"That's Gabriel," I said excitingly, "so this proves he's with the agency." I look into Thomas's eyes.

"Almost, I will make some calls after we finish with these files, to see if I can talk to his supervisor" Thomas leans closer, nudging me with his shoulder before he stands up.

"So, my Uncle is really the mastermind of The Front?" Thomas shakes his head.

"I don't think so. I think he's the man behind Project Maverick." Thomas smiles, "I think we found the key to end Project Maverick."

I smile, as my eyes gleam with excitement. I can finally go home. I'm free.

Chapter 31

The Lines

I spend the night with Thomas, searching for answers in stacks of files related to Gabriel Zottigati, and the organization called The Front. We found that The Front is a front for the MI6, and Gabriel's mission to take down an organization called Phantom. This organization has been funding drug wars around the world, and bribing Government officials and agencies around the world. The leader is unknown, until now. I spend the night looking for clues to see how my Uncle is connected, and I found nothing. But I know he is involved through someway, at least I thought.

"I found something," Thomas said sliding another file over to me. It shows a picture of a man or a woman, the photo is too grainy to clearly identify who it is.

"It looks like you found nothing." I snort and pass the file back to Thomas.

"Look in the bottom right of the photo." Thomas smiles, passing it back. I roll my eyes then look to see the letter PHT and the numbers 10/78-0098.

"What does that mean?" I look to see Thomas shrugging, "So, you found nothing."

"No, it's something we just need to find out what it is." Thomas said with excitement.

"Okay, but before we go on a wild goose chase." My voice fills with sarcasm, "We need to tell John about this."

"We can't," Thomas grabs the file again.

"Why not?" I don't understand. We need to tell him, then he knows he's going after the wrong guy.

"Because these files could be fake, Agent Rose has access to them, so she could have planted it, plus we have no proof that your Uncle is a part of the phantom." Thomas reaches across the table. His hands are warm, compared to mine which could have frozen the sun. I shift in my seat as butterflies fill my stomach. I scold myself for letting him have this kind of control over me.

"Do you really believe that?" I whisper.

"Yes," he leans over the table, lifting his hand behind my neck, pulling me into a gentle kiss. My face grows red, at the warmth of his lips, and my breath quickening. "Do you agree?"

"Okay," I whisper, my mind fuzzy. I pull away slightly for my eyes to meet his creamy chocolate eyes.

"Let's get you back into your tent, before people get suspicious." Thomas smiles, releasing the warm air we shared as he walks towards the door. I stand up, following him, when a guilty pain shoots through my heart. I know who it's for, but I also know he is away, and I need Thomas to trust me. And we have a connection. I attempt to convince myself, that Thomas and I have more in common than Luke and me. As we walk down the hallway, I hear a voice, that's medium pitch, I know it's John.

"Thomas, John is coming." Thomas looks to his right and pulls me into a supply closet. The space is claustrophobic. My back is pressed against his chest. My face is hot, as I feel his breathing become heavy. I'm glad the closet is dark at that moment. I feel his hand reach around my waist.

"Jacy, I can't reach the door knob." Thomas whispers.

"Oh, uhm, I got it." I place my hand on the knob and crack open the door, so that a sliver of light peer into the closet, shining a yellow line down my face. I glance into the hall; I couldn't see or hear anyone. "I think it's clear."

"Okay, let's go." Thomas and I step out of the closet, into an empty hallway.

"Something doesn't feel right," I say, looking down the hall. Thomas pulls out his gun.

"Stay close."

I nod, following him down the hall to a door where it opens into the lobby of the building. Thomas holsters his gun, and turns toward me to fix my hat, pulling it further over my face. Thomas's hand lingers on my shoulders, as though he's trying to compose himself and waiting for me to be ready. I nod, then he turns and walks out the door. I trail closely behind him.

"Thomas!" A woman's voice echoes across the lobby. I try to telepathically tell him to just keep walking, but he stops. I look over to see Agent Rose rushing across the floor.

"Yes?" Thomas's voice is tense, as well as his stance. I walk past him a few feet.

"John knows where The Front is." Thomas looks towards me, then back at her.

"Where?" His voice grows concerned.

"Come with me, and I'll show you." Agent Rose motions for him to follow. He looks at me and gives me an apologetic look. I give him a slight nod, then I walk out of the building into the damp air. I walk behind the tents where the woman I hit was. Now she has disappeared. I shrug and kept walking until I reach my tent. I know if I walk in there without Thomas, the guards would grow suspicious, so I dug up one of the back parts of the tent then crawled under and into my room. The fire is burning bright, and the heat in the tent feels unbearable. I take my coat off, exposing my shoulders and place it on my cot. I've been up for a total of twenty hours. My eyes feel like they could fall out and the only way to keep them in is to close them.

I see Luke standing in front of me, his smile is warm, his eyes glow, putting into a trance, like a moth to a flame. I feel his hand on mine, pulling me into him. I know it's a dream, yet I could still smell his scent of fresh sandalwood. I didn't want the dream to end. I want to stay here where it's just him and me. I pull away to see Thomas. I look into his eyes, as he pulls me into a kiss.

I wake up to the sound of clanking metal and the wind howling throughout the camp. I feel as though it's going to pick up my tent and take me to a far-off place. My tent has cooled off now, and the fire has died down. I pick up my jacket and throw it over my shoulders. I look around for wood but there's none. The guards are outside still. That means Thomas is still with Rose and John. Rose must have planted something for John to find, that would lead to the end of Gabriel's plan. This brings me to the question of what Luke and Jessica are doing? I know Gabriel has them spread the news that they are looking for Uncle Larry, but what are they doing until the final phase? Luke said he would be watching me, maybe he's in the camp also. No, that would be too risky.

"Jacy? Are you in here?" I hear Thomas's voice whisper as he enters the tent.

"Nope." I smile, putting sarcasm into my voice. Thomas turns around walking out of the tent for a couple of seconds then returns with a smile.

"What were you doing?"

"I ordered my guards to get some wood for the tent." He walks over to me, "John knows where Gabriel is, they are at a marina just outside of Southampton. We are moving out tonight."

"We? As in John, Agent Rose, you and I?" Thomas nods. I smile, this is it. The final phase.

"Jacy, can I talk to you?" Agent Rose walks in, and Thomas's face turns cold. I nod. "Alone?"

Thomas immediately turns and walks out without hesitation.

"What's up?" I study her face, which gives me a bad feeling that something bad is about to happen.

"John found Gabriel too soon. They aren't in position yet."

"What?"

"Gabriel, Jessica and Luke aren't in position yet. The team isn't ready. You must find a way to stall them. We need another day or so." Agent Rose says frantically.

"Okay, what am I supposed to do?" My mind spins trying to come up with ideas, but I couldn't. It's like a block of cement keeping me from freedom.

"You need to stall Thomas, which will stall everyone else. No one can move without Thomas's order." She says calmly, I nod still not knowing how I'm going to stall Thomas. He knows that Agent Rose is with The Front. He didn't trust anyone. I didn't know if I could convince him to wait. Agent Rose left as quickly as she came. I collapse on my bed. How am I going to do this? I'm stumped. All I know is that I need to figure something out, if I'm ever going to get back home.

Chapter 32

The File

I spend the final hours debating whether I should stall. I know that Luke as well as agent Rose is with The Front. But, I also found out that Gabriel is with the agency, and he's right, Thomas wouldn't trust the agency or him, even when he saw the files for himself. Plus, Luke's with Gabriel, and if they aren't in place then I could put Luke's life at risk and Thomas's. My mind is full of a tangle mess of deception. I didn't know what to believe, or which one to follow, my heart, or my head. My heart is telling me to stall, to make sure Luke is safe, as well as my brother and Thomas. On the other hand, my head telling me to go. If Gabriel is with the agency, they shouldn't be worried about us arriving early unless we scare away Uncle Larry. Overall, I didn't know anything, and I couldn't trust anyone.

"Are you ready?" Thomas peeks into the tent. Am I ready?

"No, I think we should wait just to make sure he is right." I have to follow my heart. I know its cliché, but it's what I have to do. I need make sure everyone will be safe. I have to make sure Luke will be safe.

"You think your brother is wrong?" Thomas is halfway in the tent now. I nod, even though I know he's right.

"I think we need to be totally sure before we go risking lives." Thomas nods in agreement. I walk over to him, grabbing his shirt down by his hip. "Let's just wait a day then if the intel doesn't change then we should go, okay?"

"Okay," his face turns a light pink, when I look at him with the same puppy eyes I use on my brother when I want an extra scoop of ice cream. Thomas leans down pressing his lips to mine. "I'll go talk to John and Agent Rose."

"Okay," I smile and thought, I need to talk to Agent Rose. "Thomas, can you send Agent Rose in?" Thomas looks down at me, with a smile that's contagious.

"Yes, what for?"

"Oh nothing important just wanted to ask her a question."

Thomas studies my face, searching for the lie, "Okay."

I relax, releasing a breath as he disappears out into the camp. I know he's suspicious, but at this point I'm not sure if I care, all I care about is that the plan goes as planned. And for that to happen I need Agent Rose to tell me everything that Gabriel is doing with Luke and Jessica.

"Thank you for stalling." Agent Rose said with relief.

"I need you to tell me everything." I snap. I didn't know what came over me.

"About?"

"About what Gabriel is having Luke and Jessica doing."

"That's need to know." Agent Rose crosses her arms.

"And if Gabriel wants his little mission to go right then I need to know," my voice fills with sass. "I'm tired of being kept in the dark."

"Look I understand. Being in the dark is hard, not knowing if what you're doing is really worth something is hard, but that's just how things operate."

I hate how sincere she sounds, like she understands what I'm going through. But she has no idea what I've gone through. The fact that my whole life is a lie and my family is lying to me. I was taken from my hometown to a foreign country, and the lives of everyone I love now lay on my shoulders.

"You have no idea what I've been through." My voice fills with anger now. "Look, all I want is a light. I need a little hope please." She stands there, staring at me for a minute. Her eyes calculating.

"Okay," she sighs. "I can't tell you everything."

"Okay." Disappointment shoots through my face.

"But this is what I can tell you," Agent Rose smiles, "Luke and Jessica are spreading the word about Gabriel so that your uncle will find him at the meeting point where John found."

"So, Luke is luring my Uncle into a trap?"

"Yes."

"Is there any way I can talk to Luke?" I smile, already knowing what her answer would be, no, but Luke is the only one I feel like I could trust on Gabriel's team.

"No," Agent Rose tilts her head. "Well maybe. I'll have to see what I can do." Excitement fills my veins at the thought of being able to talk to him. My heart is pulsing with a newfound joy.

"When can I?"

"I don't know yet, but I'll let you know when I know. And now that you stalled, I think we'll be right on schedule, and Gabriel should let Luke talk for a while." She smiles and pulls out her phone.

"Can you put it on speaker?" She nods, setting the phone down on the cot.

"Hello?" A man's voice cracks through the phone.

"Gabriel? This is Agent Rose."

"Agent Rose, to what do I owe the pleasure?"

"Jacy stalled, so everything should be right on track, sir."

"Good, Luke and I have been getting everything set. We have the guns, the men, and now all we need is Larry and Thomas."

"How is Jessica doing?"

"Good, she's still spreading the word for the trap and she is handling transportation to Antarctica." Antarctica? I look at Agent Rose who seems just as surprised as I. What's in Antarctica? I thought back through all the files I read. And none of them mentioned Antarctica.

"Okay. John wants to leave first thing in the morning."

"Perfect, and if Larry Carmichael does what I think he will do, then we got ourselves a showdown." Even though I couldn't see Gabriel, I could still see his smug smile that makes me question everything he said. "I have to go. Keep me updated okay."

"Okay," Agent Rose, stares at the phone until it turns to a long low beep. I watch her carefully as she presses the button that makes the sound stop.

"Why Antarctica?" My voice inquisitive.

"I don't know." She shakes her head, erasing the question that I could see weighing on her mind. Her eyes dart to mine, "Get some rest, you have an early morning ahead of you." And before I could say a word, she is gone.

I spend the evening pondering what Gabriel could have in Antarctica. It's a barren place, rarely any life. What could he be hiding? And why would he take my uncle to Antarctica if he's really with the agency? I'm lost and so is Agent Rose. The way she reacted when Gabriel said Antarctica makes me sympathize for her, for one reason. She is also in the dark.

Chapter 33

The Travel

I was around ten when I got my first pet, it was a goldfish named Bo. My brother Josh got it for me after I fell and dislocated my shoulder, hiking with John. I remember the responsibility of feeding it every day, changing its water once a week, and cleaning its tank. It felt like a lot at that time, but no responsibility can compare to what I have to do now. Discover who is the real crime lord and stop him. I would rather have a dog. I smile at that thought, it's zero three hundred when John comes in to get me.

"Jacy, we are leaving in five minutes." His voice makes me jump. When I open my eyes, he is gone. I trudge out of bed, throwing on the change of clothes John must have left. There's a black tank-top with light tan pants, that looks like what an explorer would wear, then as always, black cargo boots. I quickly lace them up and throw on my coat that hangs over a chair where the guards used to sit. Where are they? I look out the tent to see them standing with Agent Rose, John and Thomas under a light that seems to sway in the wind. The wind is slightly blowing, just enough to stir up the scuff of snow that rests on the ground. As Thomas's eyes find me, I smile, seeing them light up with joy. My eyes scan him up and down. Something is different, his clothing is normal, black polished boots and black military- issued pants with a true-blue colored coat. His eyes are still that milky chocolate that I could melt in if I look at them too long. His hair, that's what it is, it's shorter along the sides and the top is a little shorter than its medium length yet still long enough to swoop in the wind.

"Hey, nice haircut." I nudge Thomas flirtatiously.

"Thank you," he nudges me back, then look at John, who holds a disappointing look at Thomas then at me. I smile, knowing that what I'm about to do would annoy him.

"Thomas, am I riding with you?" I place my hand on Thomas's arm.

"You can," an embarrassed smile appears as Thomas sways towards me a little. I glance at John who looks severely annoyed now. I laugh, taking a step closer to Thomas.

"Time to go." John says harshly when he turns towards the trucks that are running.

"Which one are we in?" I ask Thomas, as he grabs my hand pulling me to the truck in the front of the convoy. His hand is warm. I couldn't help but think what if this is the last time, I got to feel his hand in mine. I shake my head; I couldn't think like that. I need to be positive. I need to stay focused.

"So I went through the files on Gabriel again." Thomas whispers as the truck starts down the road out of camp.

"Did you find anything new?"

"Yes, you know that picture that I showed you," Thomas pauses, waiting for me to acknowledge that I remember the picture, which I vaguely remember, so I nod. "Okay, I made a few calls and found out that he is with the agency."

"That's good, that means he was telling the truth," Luke is with the good guys, I smile at that thought. That means so is Jessica and Agent Rose, but my Uncle is a crime lord. I'm related to a criminal.

"Yep, it's that or the agency is corrupted. Either way I should have been read in." Thomas slid closer to me. "Anyways we still need to be careful. He's been undercover for a really long time, so I don't know if that has gotten to him."

"What do you mean?"

"I mean, the psychological stress might have gotten to him after all those years of being undercover." Thomas's voice is low. "I mean he could be a double agent now." My heart sinks as I erase the thought of Luke being with a good guy out of my mind, and back to the original thought of not knowing. I'm back to square one.

A man stands before me, his hair is a gold that is mixed with dark strips of brown that's evenly spread throughout his hair. He is tall, with a navy-blue suit that outlines his jawline framing his piercing blue eyes. I'm in a black, strapless dress that stops just above my knees, my hair is curled so that it flows down just beyond my collar bone. My cheeks grow a rose red when I feel his rough hand gently graze my forearm down to lace his finger with mine.

"Come with me," the man said, I nod and follow him to a car. And, he opens the door, I fall into a dark room.

The air is thin, and the floor is covered in ankle deep freezing water. I shiver when I splash through the water running from wall to wall trying to find an exit. When the ceiling starts to rain, drenching me. I look up to see a gray sky and four men standing over me. Then they disappear one by one leaving me alone. I look around again to see a door open letting a yellow beam of light in the room. I rush through the door into a white hallway. I'm dry now with a gun in my hand. I walk slowly down the hall when suddenly a man appears. I train my gun on him, as he walks forward, he's older and with black hair. He points the gun at me, not at the man in the suit, at Luke. He looks at me and smiles as his finger squeeze around the trigger. I leap in front of Luke.

"Jacy, Jacy. Wake up. Everything is okay." Thomas's voice is soothing, which oddly helps calm me down. What did that dream mean? I know it meant something. Is Luke going to die? Who is that man that shot Luke? Is it Gabriel? Uncle Larry? I look at my watch, it's zero seven hundred hours.

"Where are we?" I look out the window to see houses and cars.

"We are in Southampton, going to set up HQ at a building in a lot about two miles from the canal."

"Okay," I look at Thomas trying to figure out what Gabriel is planning.

"Are you okay?" His voice is filled with concern as are his eyes.

"Yes, I was just trying to figure out what The Front was planning."

"Okay," he smiles placing his arm around me. I smile, as my heart pumps faster, making my cheeks grow red. "You look good."

"Thank you, so do you." I lean into his chest.

"Well thank you." Thomas smiles, "you see that building, that's partly torn down. That's where we will set up." The building looks over a dirt lot that's fenced in, which allows only one exit. This could be a tactical advantage. The trucks drive into the lot and park as well as the other trucks. I step out with Thomas right behind me. John and Agent Rose steps out ordering the men to start hauling the equipment up inside. Thomas grabs my waist making my stomach tingle with butterflies. His hands slips off my waist as he moves me aside to go talk to John. I shake my head in embarrassment.

"I see you and Thomas have gotten very close. Good job." I jump, to see Agent Rose smiling.

"What do you mean good job?" I cross my arms

"I mean good job. I didn't think that was how you would get him to trust you, but you did. So good job." She looks at Thomas and John.

"That's not how I did it, but thanks for that." I roll my eyes. Agent Rose shrugs. "Anyways, what's Gabriel's plan?"

"He got in contact with your uncle, and they are going to meet here at eighteen hundred hours. Luke will be with

Gabriel as well as Jessica. And we will go intercept the targets once we get our intel." I nod, after tonight the nightmare will be all over. I'll get to go home. I walk to the back of the truck and grab two bags and start to haul them upstairs. Thinking, after this, I will be free from all the lies.

Chapter 34

The Final Straw

It takes hours to set up, my arms are exhausted from hauling bag after bag. John and Agent Rose seem to get along. Every now and then I would catch them laughing and talking. I couldn't help but think John didn't know what he is getting himself into. I know I didn't when I met Luke for the first time, but then again I didn't like Luke, he and Madison are together. I miss hanging out with my friends. I wonder if they even know that I'm gone. Probably not, which is a good thing. I don't want them involved in this. I know Kim and Madison wouldn't be able to handle it. But at least they would be someone to talk to. Someone I know I could trust. Unless they are also involved with Gabriel or my uncle. I shake my head knowing that would be crazy. Yet possible, considering I would never have thought John and Luke would be spies. Or that I would meet an agent from MI6. I open a long black bag to reveal a rifle. The rifle is black with folding stock and a suppressor. I look around to try and find Thomas, but instead I find Agent Rose.

"What would we need this for?" I point at the gun as though it's a snake.

"It's just a precaution, just in case it gets out of hand." She smiles, as she grabs the case and walks up the stairs. I went back to unpacking now with the thought of this operation going wrong. It can't go wrong. I need it to go perfectly. It can't go wrong, can it?

✳✳✳

Jacy hasn't left my mind since I last seen her. I've been with Gabriel and Jessica for days now, getting set up for the last phase of his plan to finally end Project Maverick and end Operation Phantom. I hate not being able to be there for Jacy and having to keep secrets from her. But, I know it's for the better. Every now and then I would get a chance to see her through the surveillance cameras we tapped into. She's always beautiful even through the static camera feed. I haven't seen her since this morning when the man that tortured me woke her up. I believe him to be her brother John, or Josh. I'm not sure. Gabriel never told me even though I asked many times. Which he ignored. Gabriel nudges me, pointing across the road at a building that is half torn down. I look through my binoculars, to see four trucks pulling up to the base of the building. Two people exit the first truck. I adjust my binoculars to see Agent Blake standing behind Jacy. Anger fills my veins, as my muscles tense. All I want to do is punch his smug face, then take Jacy way from him.

"Everything is in place. Jacy has gained Thomas's trust." Gabriel said, I give him the thumbs up as I didn't dare to take my eyes off of Jacy. "Don't worry, Luke, soon enough you and Jacy can be together while we all are in sunny Antarctica." Gabriel pats my back, as I give him a confusing look.

"Sunny?" My voice is skeptical.

"Well cold and some sun." I roll my eyes, then look back down at Jacy who is now hauling stuff into the building.

"Actually, I was thinking, after this Jacy and I can go back home." I know Gabriel wouldn't let me go, considering I knew all about his operation, and his involvement with the government. If I'm gone, I'm a liability. But it would be worth a try.

"Like a vacation?" I nod. Yes, like a vacation forever. But he didn't need to know that. When I was a kid, Gabriel taught me how to live off the grid, untraceable. And if I can get Jacy, then she would be safe. Being part of Gabriel's team apart of MI6 is too dangerous. It's great at first to get away from my family, to learn to be on my own and to be unstoppable if I need to be, and most importantly, I have nothing to protect. But now I feel like I have everything to protect. I have everything to lose. I have Jacy.

"Yes, I think that it would benefit Jacy, to have a break. Especially since she was just thrown into this life." I look at Gabriel who seems to sincerely consider my request.

"I think that would be alright. How long do you think she will need?" I smile thinking that if we had a month, we could truly drop off the radar.

"I was thinking a month, but if you need us sooner we will come."

"I think that's a good idea," Gabriel smiles, looking at his phone, "I have to go, Jessica needs me at the ship."

"Okay, I'm going to set up here," I smile, knowing I can go down and do some recon. I look over to see that Gabriel has disappeared. I look down at my phone, that has two notifications, one from Madison, the other from Jessica. I decide to ignore Madison, and open Jessica's.

'Luke make sure to set up the sniper's perch, and put explosives around the perimeter'

'Don't worry I will,' I type. I shake my head putting a black cap on and a light brown trench coat, with sunglasses. I throw my backpack on and walk down to the street. I walk across the street to the lot. There are still men hauling stuff in the building, I keep my head bowed as I set the explosives by the gates, then under an old car that's fifteen feet away from the gate. I force a limp as I walk over to building Jacy is in with Agent Rose, and Agent Blake and her brother. I place a detonator on the side of the building.

"Hey, what are you doing?" A man said. I start to cough uncontrollably.

"Sorry, sir, I was just trying to rest." I walk over to him.

"Just keep moving." The guard backs away, then disappears back within the fence. That's a close one, I nod walking away behind the building, taking off my coat and my hat, then running across the street and walking back to the building I was originally in. Once I got there, I set up the high-powered rifle, then I wait for Gabriel and Jessica. As I sit there, I look at Madison's text.

'Hey, where have you been?'

'I've been busy.' I roll my eyes.

'Oh, I see, well maybe once you're done being busy we can go catch a movie? And have you seen Jacy lately?'

'No, and look Madison, I'm sorry but I don't think I can.' how am I going to let her down? How am I going to tell her my life is too complicated for her?

"Sir?" I look up to see a man standing in the doorway.

"Yes?" I narrow my eyes.

"Gabriel is downstairs." The man said. I nod and walk down stairs. Gabriel is standing by the bar, as is Jessica. Gabriel takes a swig of drink, leaving the glass empty on the bar. I smile knowing this is it. This is the final phase.

Chapter 35

The Escape

I find myself looking out at the lot, studying the weather. The clouds hover over the mountain tops, and the sun is setting in the west over the canal. The wind has died down to a small breeze that sways my ponytail to my left shoulder. I watch the cars race by as people make their way home from work to their families. There's a building across the street with a bar in the bottom, and a diner on the other side. I watch as people pile in and flow out as the sun starts to disappear. I look around, everyone is geared up with a black commando suit and a bulletproof vest that blends in. Three throwing knives are placed in the front of their vests, a pistol holsters at their thighs, and across their chests is an M4 Carbine. I watch Thomas as he laces his shoes, and fixs his vest leaving his appearance spotless. He caught me watching and throws me a smile that shoots a shiver down my spine.

"Jacy," I look over my shoulder to see John. He holds a 9mm.

"Yes?" I said. John motions for me to follow him. I didn't know why but start to choke up with a feeling of sadness that fills my chest. I follow him to a stairwell that lead to the roof. "What's going on?"

"First, I love you. Second, I will never intentionally leave you or hurt you." His eyes form a gloss that turns his eyes a dark green.

"Stop, you're not going anywhere. You will be right down there. I will be watching you the whole time." I burst.

"Just in case something does happen, and I don't come back. You need to know this." John grabs my hands, "Josh and Mama June are with my handler, Kale Crown. I don't know where they are at. Only Kale knows, if you need them get in contact with him. Okay? Also, I have a safe."

"How do I get in contact with him? And I've already seen your safe in your room with the hidden compartment."

"The one in my room, right?"

"Yes."

"There's a slip safe in the door frame of a house in Villalba de Duero." John releases my hands letting them fall to my side.

"Which house is it? How will I know it's your house? And how do I find it, and your handler?"

"In the safe there's a card, and a phone number. And trust me, you will know which house is mine, once you see it." John looks at his watch. "It's time to go, but Jacy, don't trust anyone. I love you kiddo," John pulls me into an embrace. My eyes start to swell. He's not leaving, nothing will happen to him. I will be watching him the whole time. I won't let anything happen to you, I promise. I thought as the radio static turns on.

"Agent Carmichael where are you? It's time," A voice muffles through the static. John pulls away, with a gentle smile on his face.

"I have to go." John waits for me to acknowledge that it's okay, but it isn't.

"I'll be there in a second." John nod, squeezing my hand once before he left the stairwell. I didn't know what to do. I lean against the wall, trying to catch my breath, and my thoughts. But both seem to be out of reach. I need to be there to watch over him, I need to keep him safe. I force a deep breath then I walk out to see Thomas standing, in front of the door, looking at me. He smiles and walks over to me pulling me into him. The smell of his fresh cologne brings a certain comfort, that makes John's goodbyes seem to melt away. "Thomas?"

"Yes?"

I pulled away, so that my eyes meet his.

"I need you to watch after John. Okay?"

Thomas nods without hesitation. "Thank you."

"You're welcome," He smiles, "are you ready?"

"Nope," I smile as Thomas kisses my forehead, letting his fingers trace the back of my arm down to my hand. His fingers lace with mine, then he pulls me over to the group of men standing around a metal table.

"Jacy, you will be here keeping watch over the transaction, with Agent Rose." Thomas nods, making sure that I understand. Thomas escorts me through the group to see a rifle mounted on the table. "If you see anything, then you can talk to me through this." Thomas holds out an earpiece.

"Wait, what about the rifle?" Thomas looks at me, then at the gun as I place the earpiece in.

"Agent Rose will be behind the gun. All you have to do is look through these." Thomas hands me binoculars and smiles. "I'm going to get my men set up. Agent Rose will be with you."

I nod as he walks his men downstairs. The sun has disappeared now, leaving a crescent in the sky, and a dimly lit lot. And an eerie feeling that hangs in the air.

It's time. Agent Rose sits at my right with the gun lifted towards the lot, it begins fill with cars. Three black cars stir up the dust as they roll into the lot. I look through the binoculars, to see a parade of men step out of the cars. There are two men wearing suits and one with a briefcase. They must be the leaders. I adjust the binoculars to see who it's, the first man is an older gentleman with a heavy-set build, Uncle Larry. And to his right a younger man, it's too dark to clearly see him, but he's taller than Uncle Larry. What is in that briefcase? I look back at the gate as three more cars appear. Two men step out of the first car, the second car four men and a girl, and the third car stops in the entrance of the gate. Two men got out and step on the outside of the car, resting their guns on the car's hood and trunk.

"The one closer to us is Gabriel, the next one is Luke, and the furthest is Jessica." Agent Rose said, resting the butt of the gun on the table. I look back down at the standoff. I grab a cone-shape listening device. I point it at the men and placing the earbud in one ear, then giving the other one to Agent Rose.

"You got the girl?" The man with the briefcase said.

"Yes, she's here." Gabriel said.

"Agent Rose, what girl are they talking about?" I dread asking that question.

"You," Agent Rose said. My jaw drops. Why would my Uncle need me?

"You got the money?" Luke says.

"Yes, and there's a bonus if the girl isn't hurt." The man says.

"Okay, just one thing, why do you need her?" Gabriel asks.

"You don't need to know that." My Uncle says. Hearing his voice makes me flash back to when Luke was shot. Fear swells up in my chest. "Kid, how's the arm?"

"Better," Luke said. A low laugh escapes my lips. I look at Agent Rose, as she pulls out her phone. I look back to the lot. The man with the briefcase walks to the center where he is met with Jessica.

"Now where's the girl?" Uncle Larry said.

"Hold on we have to count first." Gabriel said as Thomas's men appears and pours into the lot like ants. I look at Agent Rose, who pulls up the rifle. I look back down, I count Uncle Larry's, men, ten. They're missing two men.

"Agent Rose, there are two men..." I stop as I feel a metal cylinder press between my shoulder blades.

"Missing? Hands up, sweetie." One of the men said, "boss we got them."

"Drop all your weapons and move slowly downstairs." The second man said. I look at Agent Rose, she nods as though telling me to do as I'm told. I place the listening device on the table along with the binoculars. Agent Rose rests the rifle on the table along with her Glock that is at her hip. The first man walks behind me pushing me down the stairs and out into the lot. Agent Rose was behind me, along with the second man.

"Boss, we found them." The man said to Uncle Larry. Thomas, Luke and John turn towards me. I look at Luke, his eyes widen with hurt.

"Jacy, sweetie, it's good to see you again." He walks over to me. I try to step back but the gun barrel dug into my back. "Agent Blake tell your men to back down, or I hurt her." Thomas looks at me, deciding whether I could take whatever is coming or not.

"No," Thomas says bluntly. The man behind me lifts the gun to my head.

"Call your men back now," Uncle Larry said. Thomas stare at him; his eyes never leave Uncle Larry.

"Thomas do it." John said. Thomas looks at John, "Alfa squad, RT."

"Good boy." Uncle Larry said as Thomas's team laid down their guns for Larry's men to take over. They move all of Thomas's men into the building then jam the doors with an iron rod. Uncle Larry makes his way over to me, lifting my chin with the barrel of his gun. Thomas and Luke flinches towards me, but Larry's men stopped them. "Oh, you two have it bad for my sweet little niece here."

Luke and Thomas narrow their eyes in sync to glare at each other before shifting their focus back to me. I look at them, not knowing what to do. Not knowing how to feel.

"What do you want?" Gabriel said. Uncle Larry motion as his men take the stock of the gun whacking him in the head.

"I wasn't talking to you." Uncle Larry said, returning a look of disgust at Thomas, and Luke. "Let me guess you both are in love." Luke stand straight up, as well as Thomas. Neither of them said a word.

"Jacy, what did you do to get these two foolish men to fall for you?" I look at him, my face stern. I didn't know what to say. All I want to do is to punch him. I start to size him up, his height, weight, strength. I could take him. But the man behind me dig the barrel deeper while the man that has the briefcase walks over to Uncle Larry and whispers in his ear. Larry's face changes from confident to what looks like concern, almost fear. What did that man say? I look over to

John. His expression is austere, his stance is offensive as though he is about to strike.

"What do you want?" John said. Thomas shoots him a look that told him to back down, but he ignores it.

"I need my little niece," Uncle Larry smiled, fiddling with his gun.

"Why?" John's voice is inquisitive, and fierce.

"Because my competitor seems to take a specific interest in her, and our family." Uncle Larry turns towards me, Luke takes a step forward. I shoot him a look that tells him I will be fine.

"So, you plan on using her to negotiate with your competitor." Thomas said, his voice is low. Larry nods, looking at his watch.

"Well, sorry to cut this short but, we need to leave before the man comes."

"The man?" I ask.

"My competitor, he wants you for something, and since he has a lot of power, I figure, I would gather some of that power myself." Larry's voice starts to build with fear. I think I need to meet this man. "Put her in the car."

"No," Luke shouts, as the man behind me starts to push me. I look at Thomas, then Luke, and John. John swings his elbow back, knocking one of Larry's men on the ground. The man that stands by my uncle raises his gun. Uncle Larry places his hand on the man's arm. The man slowly lowers his gun.

"I will get you out of this I promise." He said.

"No, you'll get hurt." I said. Luke tries to walk to me, but the guard grabs him around the collar of his shirt, pulling Luke back into him. The guard that John elbowed has blood dripping out of his nose, as he walks over and pulls John back. John shoots his elbow back again but this time the guard is ready and caught his elbow then twists it behind John's back. I look between Thomas, Luke, Agent Rose, and Gabriel trying to send the message that we should all attack at the same time. Thomas did a slight nod, as well as Luke, Gabriel and Agent Rose. As the guard starts to push me towards the car again, I lift my foot kicking backwards into his knee. He screams in pain as he collapses to the ground. I take my elbow across his face and his body goes limp. My heart is racing, I grab his gun and lift it towards Uncle Larry.

I look at John who still has a gun to his head, while Thomas, Luke, Gabriel and Agent Rose has disarmed their guards and hold them at gunpoint. Luke take his gun across the guard's face. The guard collapses to the ground in what looks like slow motion.

"Jacy, you're outnumbered." Uncle Larry said, his voice calm. I look around me, and he is right. We are outnumbered, but I know I couldn't give up. I couldn't become a prisoner again.

"That might be so, but I'm not going to go with you." I smile.

I look at Luke who aims his gun at the man who stands beside my Uncle. Luke gives me a smile. I smile back, "Now release my brother."

"No."

I look between Luke and John. I didn't know what to do or say.

"Okay," Luke says, shifting his aim over to the guard behind John.

"This got interesting." Uncle Larry said looking at his watch. "But I don't have time to see your little plan, play out." Uncle Larry lifts his gun at Thomas, while his man beside him pointed his at Luke. My heart is pounding, I couldn't think. I didn't know what to do. I know I couldn't go with him, but I also couldn't have anyone getting hurt. I need to find something. I need leverage. Then it hit me. I need to stall until the man my uncle is afraid of shows up, if he shows up.

"Now Luke!" Gabriel yells, as explosions burst around the lot. My ears ring with a high-pitched whistle. I look at Luke who has knocked out the guard that's holding John. Gabriel shoot the guard across the lot. Agent Rose disables the guard behind her and the one behind Gabriel. Agent Rose grabs me, pulling me behind the car, as bullets fly through the air ricocheting off the car. Luke slid over the trunk of the car. John follows, as well as Thomas. While Gabriel scurries around the front of the car, stirring up dust.

"We need to get out of here!" Thomas yells as he returns fire.

"No, I was thinking of building a home here!" Luke's voice is thick with sarcasm.

"Well, if you wouldn't have started to blow stuff up, we could have gotten out of here safely!" Thomas yells.

"If you would have kept Jacy safe, we wouldn't be in this situation!" Luke screams back.

"Well if you..."

"Stop! This isn't the time to argue about who did what!" I yell, "we need to work together if we are going to get out of here alive."

"Okay, what do you have planned?" Thomas says, as he lifts his gun and shoots over the car. I look from one end of the line to another; I didn't know what to do.

"I'll distract them, while you guys get Jacy out of here," John's voice is filled with anguish. I look over to see his hand covering his ribs, as blood seeps through his fingers. John rips off his vest, releasing a breath of freedom.

"No, John you're bleeding." My voice cracks, and my eyes fill with tears. I crawl over to him. "We need to get you out of here." I look over to Thomas, and Luke. "Help me!"

"Kiddo, even if I do get out of here. I won't make, it." his voice is choked, his eyes water, "I love you."

"Don't say that, you will survive." I look at Luke pleading for help, but he just sits there, with his head hangs low.

"Jacy, I will stay with him." Gabriel said.

"No, I can't leave him." I cover his hand with mine. His breaths start to quicken and then become shallower. I couldn't leave him. He is my brother. He is the guy that taught me how to climb a building. He taught me how to defend myself against bullies in the school yard. He's my family. I can't leave him. He can't leave me. I didn't know what I would do without him. I feel a hand linger on my shoulder.

"Jacy it's time to go," Thomas's voice is soft. John begins to shake as he tries to stay alive. I shake my head.

"No, I can't leave him." Tears pour down my face, as the heavens open soaking my clothes.

"Jacy," John lifts his hand to my cheeks. My hand covers his as I tilt my head into his hand, "Jacy, you need to know that…" John starts to cough, "Our dad… he's…" John voice trails off as his body became limp.

"John? John stay with me." His hand falls from my face, "John?"

"Jacy, he's gone." Thomas said. I close my eyes, thinking, you can cry later. Right now, you need to save these people, you need to finish Project Maverick. I sit here for a minute, calming myself down, trying to find a way to save everyone.

"Ceasefire!" I yell, "ceasefire!" The sound stops to leave the smell of gunpowder in the air. I raise my hand up, standing up slowly. Uncle Larry has his gun trained on me. "I'll go with you, as long as you promise to leave everyone here alone and unharmed." Uncle Larry looks over at his man, as though he's truly considering it.

"You won't resist?" He asks.

"I won't resist." I said, as I slowly walk around the back of the car. Uncle Larry signals for his men to come get me. They place my hands behind my back restraining them. I bow my head as they drag me to the car. I look back over my shoulder to see Luke standing. His blue eyes shined through the dim lights. I smile, hoping that it will comfort him. I don't know whether leaving is stupid or honorable. Either way I didn't care. All I want is for Luke, and Thomas to be safe, and now they are. I sit in the back seat where Uncle Larry and what appears to be his right-hand man has joined me.

"You're doing the right thing." Uncle Larry said, as the car begins to move. Am I? At this point I thought I am, but I'm not sure. I look out the window and see Luke, he holds a device in his hand. I grab the seat belt locking it in place. Everything seems to move in slow motion as a blast shook the ground and the front of the car lifts into the air. My body slams against my seatbelt, as I hang upside down. I can't see except for a blurry blob prying open the door.

"Jacy, I got you." His voice muffles as he helps me out of the car, catching me before I hit the glass-covered roof. I wrap my arm around him. I feel blood run down the side of my head. He rushes me out of the lot and towards the canal. I look back to see blobs fighting blobs. The sound of sirens travels through the air. I reach back motioning to turn back but his grip tightens. "Jacy, we have to go."

"I need to help them." I slur.

"They can take care of themselves." He says, pulling me into him. Pain travels through my body, as my head throbs. My foot drags across a metal ramp. An over powerful smell of fish hit my nose. I force one eye open as the other one is swollen shut. I look over to see him handing what looks like the captain, a roll of money.

"You can set her over there and help me kick off from the dock." The captain says.

"Okay." He said as he brings me over to a corner and sets me down in a pile of what feels to be netting. I try to sit up, but the pain keeps me on the ground. "I'll be right back."

"Okay," I mumble. The rain has lightened up now. Only a slight mist covers my cheeks. I close my eyes, and tears began to seep through the corners as I think back to John.

"Jacy, stay awake, okay?" My eyes shoot open, to see a blurry face. I blink rapidly as the image became evident.

"Luke?" I say. He nods, with a smile. While he combs my hair away from my face. My smile fades when I shiver, Luke's eyes grow concerned. Then he lifts me into his body, giving me a comforting warmth. I'm not sure where we are going, or how long I would be gone this time. All I know, is that I'm safe with Luke. I close my eyes, letting the world fade away, leaving me in a world where the truth burns bright and the darkness disappears.

Tessa L. Gatz